AMERICAN PASTIME

Angelique Pesce

AMERICAN PASTIME

Angelique Pesce

Woodhall Press | *Norwalk, CT*

Woodhall Press, 81 Old Saugatuck Road, Norwalk, CT 06855
WoodhallPress.com

Layout artist: LJ Mucci

Library of Congress Cataloging-in-Publication Data available

ISBN 978-1-949116-79-3 (paper: alk paper)
ISBN 978-1-949116-80-9 (electronic)

First Edition

Distributed by Independent Publishers Group
(800) 888-4741

Printed in the United States of America

American Pastime is a work of fiction. Names, characters, places, incidents, and dialogue are products of the author's imagination or are used fictitiously. Where actual institutions or locations and real-life historical or public figures appear, the situations, incidents, and dialogues concerning those entities, places, and persons are entirely fictional and are not intended to describe actual events. In all other respects, any resemblance to actual events, locales, or persons, living or dead, is entirely coincidental.

The more I study science, the more I believe in God.

—Albert Einstein

True or False?

To the memory of children like Adam Walsh, the first child murder victim I learned of in my youth watching the media program *A Current Affair* with Geraldo Rivera. I believed history should never repeat itself. And to all the children who have suffered and still suffer today from violence at the hands of strangers, false persecution, violence from bullying, violence from parents, violence in their homes, violence in the streets, and now violence in their high schools. Time to make a change. Listen.

CHAPTER 1

Raindrops pooling in concentric circles down a Bronx sidewalk in New York. I, God, curiously looked down from the heavens toward the planet and fixed my eyes on the heart of one young man named Adam Weakley, thirties, looking grungy, face not revealed, wearing a baseball hat, drifting through the city neighborhood.

A homeless Vietnam vet begs for change with pennies in his cup. "Thank you for your service," Adam says to the vet, tossing him a bill.

Adam recalls his own veteran father, his words abusive. "You are nothing, Adam," he would say. "You will never amount to anything. You're a loser." He was an abused kid. Even his friends were harsh to him. As far back as then, I decided to watch over him. I loved his crazy ideas about life, culture, the things humankind has created like art, education, law, economy, architecture, celluloid, and Republicans and Democrats alike. He thinks about what the world still needs, how to get it to stop breaking down like a car and how to be well oiled like a machine, fix what's wrong with it if at all, and, if possible, make what's right about it even better, or even better than that, last forever for love. Yes, he was a hopeful romantic and I wondered if he heard me at all, but today I was about to change all of that. Today, I decided to have a conversation with Adam at a baseball stadium in New York.

As he walks, Adam contemplates the war in Iraq, his American culture, the fast-food churches of capitalism relied on for the dollar that reads "In God We Trust" over the pyramid, and whether the velocity of the exchange of them born out of a necessity for people that is real and true must insist that places they are traded remain pure for the benefit of people and not subjugated by fraud and strongholds that can undermine the economy's health. He thinks about his past, present, and future, and how economists have argued that money is raw and heartless without recourse or guilt and thinks it needs a reface, as countless Wall Street types flutter by. Money cannot be sociopathic. You can bend a number, like 1 or Al'eph, into a tree or a human being. And I am 1, Al'eph. He thinks it needs to be made, earned, and spent with love in mind.

Adam stops in front of Yankee Stadium, a towering circular ancient dinosaur erected to celebrate baseball, America's favorite pastime. This would be one of its last years before it's replaced by a bigger, brighter, newer surround-sound stadium. The blueprints have been drafted, contracts signed, and the ground broken. Adam is in Highbridge, the poorest neighborhood in the United States, and he wants to take it over. He wants to build the new Yankee Stadium down the block by 2009.

Checking his watch—thirty minutes till game time.

Adam enters the coliseum. As he strolls through the arched hallway, he sees a stadium bar facing the dugout. A red, white, and blue neon sign blinks "Yankees" over its doorway, on and off, on and off. After some time Adam steps inside.

Visible are the remnants of decades past, the memorabilia like layers of a pastry cake, perfectly framed on the bar walls with autographed pictures on top of baseball cards of long-gone famous players.

The patrons line the bar like New York City pigeons on the ledge of a bridge suspended over a river of faces staring back at Adam as he strolls through space to grab a seat.

A female bartender, in her forties and wearing a fringed cowhide leather vest, looks up from her cash register to see Adam reflected in the mirror in front of her, seated. She turns away from the mirror to see her new customer in the flesh waiting for a drink.

The bartender asks, "What'll it be, cowboy?"

Without looking up, Adam tilts the brim of his black baseball cap up to say hello and responds, "A beer. Whatever you have will be fine," and places a hundred-dollar bill down. Living the dream, but it was not too long ago when he wasn't.

A Budweiser coaster is put down in front of him, followed by a pint. The head foamed up like lava over the brim and down its sides. He looks at pennies left on the bar next to him and ponders the value remaining there stacked, like the green light at the end of the dock in F. Scott Fitzgerald's *The Great Gatsby*, like hope waiting to be earned. The only question is where is he going to put it?

Reaching for a pen sticking out of his back pocket, Adam begins to write on his notepad the words "American Pastime" and recalls the childhood baseball game where his life changed forever. At the time a book titled *The Panda's Thumb* taught him everything he knew to be true about evolution. It made him want to take over his own life and his neighborhood and help it evolve. Adam writes for thirty minutes about *that* game:

"Sitting at the edge of my bed in 1986 in a sparsely decorated room, staring down at a hole in one of my cleats, the kind a poor kid would have, I poked my big toe through a tear a few times while waiting to leave for my baseball game.

"Only twelve years old, I felt like I was being watched as I held my baseball glove and ball. The glove's lace was weathered down to a fray from the once oiled-smooth skin it was threaded with."

God narrates, "For me, even as far back as then, watching Adam was something of a job description. The thread. It's always used to signify time fraying away, it's linear, flexible, able to bend around back onto itself like a Möbius loop, always connected, never future, always now, yet always aging to the person touching it. Time. It is relative. Time never ages. People age. Generations count it to organize. Why? Could only be progress. Time does not require counting it. People do.

"As far back as then, Adam was somewhat of a work of art to me, made of dirt and dust and binary code. His DNA was like a computer program, and at this point he was very simple, like C plot. He wanted his words to be shared with others if they could, something his own time line would be too short to accomplish. He wanted to build into a space where even if he, the thinker, no longer existed, his thoughts would remain, and so he wanted to write a book and build a home, Beit. He wanted to write and build something that lasted forever like the Alphabet. Alphabet means one home, Al'eph Beit. Language was created for people to communicate with one another. That kind of clarity causes world peace, one home, in union for people to live. He hoped his book and home would reflect that. The fact that language exists is proof that peace is our future."

He wanted his home to be a building for others to visit. His Taj Mahal to the community. So he set his heart on a rebuild of Yankee Stadium. *A baseball game is a good analogy for life*, he thought. Its purpose is fun. Life is more than a game, but a game is good to show rules versus empirical law. A game's empirical value is strength. Sometimes it's intelligence that is needed, sometimes it's endurance, sometimes it's physical. Knowing when either, neither, or some combination of these things gives a win is its purpose. What rules can be extracted from David and Goliath? What science can be learned from that same story? And what's the difference between rules and empirical law?

Adam's writing continues and I listen:

Fingering the frayed strand he stands up and takes a deep breath, resolute.

"Here we go. . . ." he huffs as he grabs *The Panda's Thumb* off his nightstand and exits the room, slamming the door shut behind him.

God says, "I couldn't wait to hear what he was going to think next that day and so I stayed with him. Discontent was evident in his noisiness."

Now outside, the maple trees I gave him framed the path to his baseball game, lining the street to the fence bordering their small-town baseball field. Their leaves in full bloom waxed and waned like a crowd eager to feel children's feet kick handfuls of dust to settle on their bark just like that above their gargantuan roots hinged like knees in the ground.

The pitcher's mound, looking ruddy and low, did not have dirt replenished on it for too many seasons now. No tax money free for its need or aesthetic.

With a bird's-eye-view I stare at the entire field and its players as Adam crosses the diamond into the holding pen to take a seat and wait his turn.

Adam continues to write:

"Mother Earth's green fields shining. The sun with the boys was always rising. Happy as they were young. Now, for once only, as the day would come to a close, time would tire our innocent bodies with age and lost enthusiasm.

"In the field the left outfielder, JD, twelve years old, with a wad of Big League Chew crammed in his mouth, stands completely upright, ignoring his baseball stance, leaning to one side, arm impatiently placed on his hip. 'C'mon, let's get this guy out,' he whines. Tired, he looks to his teammates for some support.

"Parents sit in the bleachers, a kaleidoscope of shoe laces and knobby knees pinstriping horizontally the pastoral setting visible between their seats, some anxiously check their watches. They prayed its end, for some-one to win, as sighs were exhaled, and each fixed their eyes at their feet. Some cleats dissolving into dust, irreplaceable by their parents financial constraints, others shiny and new like diamonds on the soles of their feet."

I, Adam, turned my attention to the umpire, thirty-five years old, calling the game's shots, cupping his hands in front of his mouth to create a funnel, a cone with his hands for his booming voice like a sonar tunnel to our eardrums, which were pounding from our heartbeats and windswept from our lost breaths.

"*You'rrrre out!*" the umpire bellows to the player up at bat who didn't get a chance to run the bases. And it was *my* turn to bat.

The out player walks off from the plate with his head hanging in defeat.

The coach, an ominous character with a baseball hat and uniform, turns toward the bench and bellows "*Weakling*, you're up!" calling me by my wrong name.

I possess no athletic ability, wearing thick nerdy glasses sitting at the end of the bench reading the science book I brought from home entitled *The Panda's Thumb*, a book about survival of the species, evolution, and natural selection, I look up surprised. I hand the book to Tommy, a player who is sitting next to me, eyes wide shut, startling him awake. I mutter to myself, "*Shiiiiiit*," and against my free will I rose from the dead to walk to home plate.

The coach, a whale of a man, roused me as I walked. "Let's go, *weak-ling*! I ain't got all day!"

I shuffle solemnly to the plate until my footprints find the steps left in the sand by Coach's shoes. My feet are considerably smaller than his and don't even reach the top of Coach's footprints. I step into each footprint left by Coach, disturbing no sand to their shape.

I feel as if I am being led to my own public execution by humiliation.

Under my breath I correct Coach. "It's *Weak*-ley, *asshole*. Looking up at him I say, "My last name, it's Weakley, not Weakling," but he doesn't hear me.

As I step to the plate I feel like I am being watched by an omniscient being. With infinite knowledge, watched. With benevolence, watched. And I can tell my whole life is about to change. I could hear a pin drop.

My feet are planted on home plate, whose white trapezoid reflects back at me like a blank piece of paper, a shade of white but covered in the game's dust. My emotions are like the Dead Sea. The sand bordering home plate wafted into the sole of my broken cleat, but this time no big toe stuck out.

I looked up at the park lights, paid for by our town hall, and recall the day Mayor Neil, arms longer than his hips like Ichabod Crane in Sleepy Hollow's Headless Horseman legend, cut a blue ribbon the day they were installed and read a dedication:

"For the children of this village, may their games and futures be bright."

Those lights shined like the rays of the sun. Love is like the sun, strong at its core, its rays shine everywhere and you grow. This day the park lights shined, linearly spreading out their rays from their electric core bulbs, lighting the field ablaze for me to run. Like UFOs in the sky, they lit my run brightly.

The opposing team teased me by calling, chanting, "*Nobatta nobatta nobatta*."

I close my eyes, take a deep breath, shaking off the dust from my cleats, and the words of the kids taunting me spoke. I think of the park lights and wonder why coach still has not taught these kids not to taunt me. And I thought of my father. And I thought about how fireworks on the Fourth of July were supposed to sound like guns and bombs. And I prayed this moment's end. The father and the fire. About leaving home. The mayor and his words.

The twelve-year-old pitcher on the mound winds up his arm and throws the first pitch before I even blink. It is thrown near my head. I automatically swing clumsily and fall on my tailbone to the ground, the thud tossing my eyeglasses off my face. I am blind.

My teammates mutter disappointment in me. The other team laughs and laughs and laughs at me.

Coach, standing at third base, kicks the dirt in frustration.

I get up and pick up my glasses, now covered in sand; they resemble an hourglass that never had the chance to hold its time. I brush the dirt off and look down the third-base line at a blurry coach. Determined, I place the dirty glasses back on and get back in the batter's box, seeing best as I can.

Suddenly I hear excited shouts. "Go Adam! Go Weakley, go!" Calling me by my right name, the sound is divine. Love. Evangeline, a sweet-faced, pig-tailed ballerina, leotard-wearing girl-next-door, watches me up at bat and cheers me on. I glance at her. She waves eagerly. The sunlight shining through her fingers spins like the blades of a fan, sunlight haloing her fingertips as they rock and roll back and forth like the counter of a metronome on its fastest staccato. I become dizzy.

Too shy to reciprocate the attention, I look down at my feet planted on home plate still reflecting back at me like a blank piece of paper. I wait for the second pitch, like a second chance, a second bite at the apple, a second crack at the bat, and I travel out of my body to a bird's-eye view as if I am having a near-death experience. I float. The audio goes silent up here until, like a boomerang, I am returned back into my body like a pebble in a slingshot. The plate now once again under my feet still a shade of white covered in the game's dust and sand.

My heart rose and fell to the pounding of my breath against its chest plate, setting my lungs off in motion like a typhoon giving rise to the butterflies in my belly. Yup, I was in love. A feeling so nauseating only my hind legs held me up. I heard my heartbeat vibrate in my eardrums to the rhythmic pattern of her name. Evangeline. *Thump*. Evangeline. *Boom*. Evangeline.

The second pitch comes. Prepared, I close my eyes, and this time I do not swing, missing the ball all together. All strategy. Not a good ball at all but no one knows.

The umpire calls, "*Striiikkke twwoooo!!!*" as his voice echoes into my blank stare. My eyes now open.

The coach, unable to control his frustration, roars like a lion from the sidelines understandably but altogether clueless, "Damn it, what the *hell* ya waitin' for! They don't come better than that! Now, c'mon, keep your eye on the damn ball and hit one *outta* here!" he says, pointing to the sky. *You don't just hit anything*, I think, and ignore him altogether.

The pitcher, Ron, with a determined look that only Atlas would hold when he held up the world on his back, is my fair opponent. He knows what he wants and he is all I care about. He shakes off several signs from the umpire, waiting for a fastball. Ron, seeing the sign he's been waiting for, smiles a knowing smile as he winds his pitch like a windmill in Amsterdam and we are about to exchange our currency. Peer to peer. Ear to ear. Connect. Communicate.

Needing pause. Focus. My eyes closed again. Darkness. Pitch black. Loud cheers muffled together in my ears. I settle myself. The beating sun pulling beads of sweat under the brim of my black baseball cap. My facial expression is determined and fierce, as the jeers "*Nobatta nobatta nobatta*" continued to echo. I ignore everything. Silence.

Tommy, the player sitting in the bullpen with my science book, is now near the sidelines chanting like the brokers on the floor of the New York Stock Exchange excited for a buy low, sell high, and I am pleased to wake to their voices.

I steady my breath. Open my eyes. The red, white, and blue threaded ball straight in front of me. I concentrate. Clench the bat, my knuckles turn white from the grip. I blink.

Ron, the pitcher, releases the ball with the speed of a rocket ship coming at me like the big bang about to happen.

My arms spring into motion, sending impulses through my body. My muscles now animate, married to the sign of the ball in my eyes through dusty lenses. Like a vessel being filled by the human spirit, like a celestial magnet between the ball and the bat. I take a giant swing. The only sound heard is the *crack of the bat. . . .*"

A bell rings back in the stadium bar. Adam is startled out of his writing. The bartender reminds the customers and Adam game time is about to begin.

Done writing for now, he rises from the stool, gets his change, grabs his messenger bag and notepad, sticks his pen behind his ear, thumbs the ticket stub stuck in his chest pocket, and leaves, ready to watch the game at the stadium.

Now inside the ballpark, the stadium's bones are like the Rome Coliseum arcs, like an amphitheater. A circle for people to stare back at each other eye-to-eye, ear-to-ear, to connect, communicate, with a pit in its center like a Big Apple to grow from its dirt mound a baseball field covered diamond for the players to play ball. This field is nothing like his childhood baseball field, and he is grateful. *Shanti. Shanti. Shanti* for the game he is about to receive. Adam inhales it all in, still recalling the young ball player he was. He can't believe he's a part of the new drafting team in New York City that's going to rebuild this stadium. His Taj Mahal is about to be achieved. Watching this game will be his last in its old bones, and it will be a special one.

With a bird's-eye-view I, God, stare at the entire field as its pro players cross the diamond into the holding pen, and I get ready to have a conversation with Adam, to break my silence about life and his thoughts.

Adam finds his seat in the bleachers. Slabs of gray concrete like the kind Pompeii housed are lined with blue plastic chairs. He takes a seat, places his notepad on his lap, and resumes writing.

He pauses to glance around like an artist looking for inspiration. He notices a portly man in a business suit, an attractive woman wearing a tank top with a lotus tattoo on her shoulder, a man in a coach's uniform, and other usual city folks happily mingling together at the game. He memorizes their geometry for a later literary time or reference as all artists do, like Leonardo da Vinci taught me to do for still-life painting.

Below on the field the game is about to begin. The scoreboard is set to double zeros and waits with electric current to be moved.

I, God, seeing Adam seated, decide to take the seat next to him. It is time. We sit side-by-side, ear-to-ear, ready to connect, communicate, our profiles stacked up like pennies next to each other, waiting for the game to begin, and there is hope.

The game-commencement horn is blown, the stadium lights illuminate as the night sky fades to a purple haze. It's the color heard through Jimi Hendrix's guitar playing at Woodstock and memorialized in that beer by the same name sold up in the Mount Vernon comfort-food restaurant the Bayou. The American flag flies high, and the players line up with hands over their hearts as the National Anthem plays till its end and the umpire screams "*Play ball!*" The first player is up to bat, but what is that? A broadcast into the stadium comes from the Giants' baseball team arena in San Francisco.

The Yankees have been asked to leave their hearts in San Francisco, where Barry Bonds, just like that, stands at home plate waiting for a pitch. Rumor has it he's aiming to break the world record for the most career home runs. The record is held by Hank Aaron of the Atlanta Braves, who achieved 755 home runs in 1974, and before that it was held by none other than Yankee legend Babe Ruth in 1935. Today in the Bronx, history is the target on the stadium screens. Barry Bonds, Mr. Bonds, the Barry Bonds, stands at home plate and Adam recognizes his face. The determination. The connection between him and the pitcher as the pitched ball hurdles toward him and he slices the ball out of the ball park. Communication.

A few game regulars watching the game at the end of the aisle suddenly break into cheers.

Adam looks up into the sky shown on the big screen, the ball soaring off of the field into the bleachers, then back down again to see the famous Giants baseball player Barry Bonds already trotting around the bases, pristine and shining in celebration of his 756th home run against the Washington Nationals. It was a record-breaking run and the year was 2007. Hank Aaron's record was hereby broken at last and all the New York Yankee players and fans turned to watch history being made.

The announcers in their boxes can be heard going into a frenzy discussing the event. The television cameras are pointed toward the bleachers where a fan catches the winning ball. Fans' faces are hollering into the air and they're jumping up and down in their seats like Slinkys, celebrating the shattering time.

A man sitting next to Adam and me, disheveled, in his sixties, nudges Adam and says, "Wow, would ya look at that? Someone just caught themselves a fortune." The man follows the baseball with his eyes on the screen. Adam grins at the man and watches as the record-breaker game ball is waived high above the head of its catcher in the bleachers. Adam thinks . . . fortune. He laughs and thinks *How belittling. I mean destiny, but what is the difference between fortune and destiny? Everything.* Adam begins to recall his childhood again, his father, and the handkerchief he carried in his back pocket.

I, God, still seated on the other side of Adam, whisper unto him, "Nice American pastime, baseball is," in contemplation of Bonds's victory. Adam, upon hearing me, takes a look at me seated next to him wearing a blue jumpsuit uniform. He smiles and sees tucked into my back pocket is a burgundy rag. He stares at me, and I grin ear to ear. Contact.

I, God, watch Adam. He turns back to the game in front of us. I hear his thoughts fade into a sunrise over a quiet suburban street where all the houses look the same, each car is neatly parked in each driveway, and each lawn is perfectly groomed. Adam begins to reflect on his childhood. I, divinely inspiring, share my thoughts with Adam to see if he can hear me. I whisper in his ear again the following:

"America's time passed, till April made its way. I said, 'Let there be baseball,' and there was. Lilacs sprouted from the earth under your feet, Adam, unveiled from their long dead sleep, and I watched you, your beautiful DNA, like a computer program to me, my language like binary code, a series of zeros and ones, and I saw you *grow*."

Adam looks up at the man. "Wow, do I know you?" I, grinning, say yes. Adam laughs. "Clearly, but what is your name?" I reply, "God."

The scoreboard now lights up 0-1 home.

Adam looks at me and says, "Wow."

I, God, say "I *know*," and continue.

"I saw the children, Adam, happy with you, playing, running from their stuffy houses, little feet naked in the grass, running. Away from their homes, away from their mothers, out from beneath the trees, forgetting the dark shadows at night, they ran naked and played, kicking handfuls of dust, singing, 'Take me out to the ball game, take me out with the crowd, buy me some peanuts and Cracker Jacks. I don't care if we ever get back, home.' They never wanted to go anyway. To me, Adam, it was paradise. Never mind what this fan just said to you about 'catching a fortune,' ignore him altogether." And I grinned, hoping he would catch on that I was like an agent in the Secret Service with a wiretap to his thoughts. I waited for him to respond.

Down on our Bronx stadium field, the frenzy of the record-breaking score has passed and the scoreboard reads 0-1 here, bases loaded with legs ready to gallop to their next base. The game is on.

Adam, I am proud to report, catches my drift. Cautious, he says, "So you saw me as a *child*?" He looks at the burgundy rag in my back pocket again.

God, "Yes. And I want to have a conversation. All right?"

Adam responds, "*Sh-sh-sure*, God."

"Don't be scared, okay? You were a spirited kid. Not a bad kid at all. Do you remember?"

Adam glances at his notepad to see the name Evangeline. "People say the butterfly effect is random but it's not, Sir, is it?" he asks, ignoring my question altogether.

God, smiling, pats Adam's back. "Ah, young love. You had it all then, huh, Adam?"

Adam looks up at me, knowing I have seen the name Evangeline on his notepad. "You knew all along what that pounding in me would bring . . . *nothing.*"

God replies, "You mean that day at your own childhood baseball game?" then pauses. "I know the path of butterfly wings and every ripple they create. Chaos is *not true.*"

Adam says, "That's a detailed design human beings just can't seem to explain yet. If chaos does not exist, then we can calculate the future. Like I could at that childhood baseball game, it changed my life forever."

Adam looks up at the field lights. "I became solemn at the plate. My heartbeat humbled up and it was as if I was standing at the edge of an ocean and realized my size for the first time. I laughed in my mind so hard at the ridiculous thought of setting myself up for anything but acceptance of my capacity at that moment, in that time on home plate. A rainstorm decidedly rumbled in the distance. Failure no longer existed," he said, looking toward God for acknowledgment, eyes tearing. "But reality remained. I ignored the thoughts of my father, the bullying of my peers, the problems I could not fix at my age: war, crime, pain, and whatever my capability would be up at bat, which would be good enough I told myself, and it was the right advice. I would let my David live as best he could in front of Goliath. What freedom."

"Sounds like fearlessness," God responds.

Adam inhales. "That moment, it changed my life forever. I felt home, at last acknowledging that I was the mere size of one single drop of rain in a space as large as an ocean. And the fun of the game took hold of me. The sheer love of it, and it was the right . . ." He pauses. "No, it was the *only* proper motivation for me at that age. I was in charge, it was my will that mattered." Adam pauses, again recalling that day. "...and you sent me that rainstorm didn't you?"

God knowingly smiles yes, "There are *no accidents*, Adam."

The crowd in the bleachers interrupts the conversation and breaks into a roar. They give a standing ovation. Bases loaded. The night sky has settled in as the game below continues at Yankee Stadium.

Adam reflects, "I took a giant swing with the force of two men that day at my childhood game as Ron the pitcher hurled that fast ball at me. And the crowd of parents, not mine, and the children who teased me went silent. Contact. That ball soared into the dimming skyline toward center field. Success. I was shocked. I grinned from ear to ear. My face opened like a lotus. And I ran toward first base as thunder began to roll. But I had no idea the rain would come. *Destiny*."

God, pleased with Adam's decision to talk about destiny, says, "I watched you round first, lightning striking. Your face glowing in triumph, the clean green fresh blades of grass crushing beneath your cleats until their hydration spilled back into the earth below. You ran, legs pumping like a horse for home."

Adam responds, "And a glorious home it was, no person manning it. Like a clear, peaceful, unprotected target ready for the taking all my own. Home plate. But the storm was coming . . . *and I thought of Evangeline.*"

God agrees. "Your heart beat to the sound of her name, Evangeline."

Adam recalls, "Our friendship grew between middle school and high school. I remember one night laying on my bed, around sixteen years old in high school, always thinking about her. My favorite book slung over my chest. It was the night before her life changed *forever*, I think and one *I will never forget.*"

God, "*Forever* is a long time. What book is it that was your favorite?" Adam laughs. "What's that? My high school yearbook, you mean?" He pauses and says, chuckling, "It replaced *The Panda's Thumb.*"

God says, "Your high school yearbook. Ironic, a book that lasts *forever.* A biopic book. What a catalog of stories, of time, of images, of people with quotes, of autographs from friends, of teachers who inspired you, of hopes locked in fixed form that remind you of where you were. Ac Fui I was there, maybe to allow you to never feel alone, to remind you of who you are. *Forever.* What a book of love. I know a book like that too. I have a favorite page, but I'll never tell. . . ."

Adam laughs. "Mine was open to a class photo of Evangeline every night during senior year. I didn't have glasses anymore then and used to cover my ears with headphones in my room blasting music to drown out the world, or just my parents' arguing. My hair was long and tucked under a navy 'White Sox' baseball cap cluttered with buttons reading 'The Clash' and 'NYHC.' I was like the adopted son of a metropolis New York City long established without me." Adam touches his own plain black baseball cap while reminiscing.

He continues, "Living with my father, Donato, the Greek immigrant he was called, was like living with a wild boar. The Vietnam War stole his innocence but he'd try to get it back with love."

His thoughts trail off like a zoetrope for me to watch. In a white clapboard house, Adam sits in his memory a teenager, the bottom of his frayed jeans slung under his heels. The door to his room opens, shedding some light from the hallway, increasing the volume of the cursing from his dad below. The year was 1992.

Adam recalls, "My mother, Susan, a native-born American, like a ghost roamed in and out of my room formless and soundless to me thanks to the headphones over my ears that blasted the music of the heavy thrashing guitar sounds I loved from my generation's favorite bands—Van Halen, Soundgarden, and Pearl Jam to name a few. It was my Do Not Disturb sign."

Susan is a boyish woman. She had five sisters. They were like the characters in Louisa May Alcott's *Little Women* and all the boys loved them. They were Irish, Italian, Navajo, and African. Beautiful. The family had been here since before the Civil War, and when it came time, they fought for Lincoln. Fought for freedom.

Adam continues, "But my father does not know how to be a better man with better visions than the Vietnam War he left behind, than the body-bag duty he was assigned, than the Agent Orange he held in his arms in the 1960s. Immigrants from Greece. His great Grandpa Dante looked at the Parthenon everyday. Dad was the second generation born here, and all the men he knew enlisted in the army. From Athens to Albany. Government was in his blood. God bless America."

Adam shakes his head and says, "And even worse, my mother can't see past her bitter visions of waving grains of wheat, large mansions, and fancy cars they can never afford, like something out of a Talking Heads video asking every day 'How did I get here? This is not my beautiful house. This is not my beautiful life.'"

God responds, "Do you think these things, like houses and cars, are distractions for people? If you had a choice, what would you want to build, fancy cars or paradise? There is nothing wrong with these things *if they speak to me or to you.* I may have built you, but you built these things. Build what you love."

Adam says, "I think what we build says something about us. When we build distractions, we lose. We should build something that looks like love. My dad loved the idea of love, but the war was his, and my mom's unemployment hers, and so the things she could not buy consumed her. We definitely built those things war and unemployment. Who wouldn't need distractions from that? My father would sit in quiet contemplation, hair in a ponytail like some kind of protester, staring at a single red rose on the mantle of the fireplace he built with his own hands in the living room. He'd bring one red rose home every Friday night like some kind of fairy tale, hoping it would speak of his love, and Mom never said thank you. What a sympathetic villain he was, living with him was like living with Lucifer in Milton's *Paradise Lost*. And what they chose to build was not love at all, but how I wish they had."

Adam glances around at the stadium, the players, the ticket holders. "That's why I want to rebuild this place, Yankee Stadium. For the love of the game and life. I see love here."

Where does one go at Adam's age to find peace? Maybe buried into the pages of his high school yearbook or in the sounds of his generation. Is love there?

God says, "You'll do a great job, I am certain, Adam. I have seen places where love is built and I think it leads to paradise. I wonder where we would be if the United States had ratified the Geneva Convention, the Doctrine on Human Rights after World War II, whether the Vietnam War would have gone down the same way. The stadium should definitely help people connect. Communicate."

Adam, "To answer your question, guess the houses, cars, and wars are mere distractions from a true endeavor toward paradise. Definitely better to build paradise."

A mother bounces her baby on her lap a few rows below us. Adam notices the baby's playful smile.

God asks, "Why do you think people do things they are not happy with or don't like?"

"Not good listeners," Adam replies.

The large stadium screens show a pitch thrown to bat. The smiling crowd cheers the players to win.

"So what do you think the cure is for unhappiness?" God asks.

Adam replies, "Learning to listen. To others and to ourselves."

"That sounds like it could build love and peace," God says.

Adam glances at the baby's face, then looks around the stadium at the people. Banners fly with names of business sponsors around them.

American Express. Ford. Pringles. Speech and capitalism. Earning, buying, and sustaining is *love*. Preventing that is *not*.

The big screen recaps the play, then focuses cameras on the people. The ticket holders now stare at each other on the screen.

God, hearing Adam's thoughts, says, "Funny, makes me think about that rule not to steal fruit from the tree of knowledge. Do you think I ever would have eventually shared that fruit with people if they had listened and not taken it on their own? Maybe they did not love *me*."

Adam says, "I could see why you ask, but we'll never know."

"Right," God answers.

Both continue staring at the screen.

Adam says, "Thank you for that *love*."

God replies, "You're welcome. People can make a conscious effort to improve the things that need it if they *listen*, Adam. Keep listening. We shouldn't have to hide our eardrums under your headphones *forever*." He smiles.

Adam grins.

God says, "*Do what you love Adam. Build what you love. Be a great listener.*"

Adam looks around the stadium and contemplates the new one to come in his blueprints.

God says, "That night at your house, after the noise subsided from your dad below, I *listened* to your heart."

I had a bird's-eye-view of Adam's face that night in 1992. He was staring at the ceiling contemplating the rooftop above and the constellations outside in the night sky. Ursa Major and its Big Dipper, Ursa Minor and its North Star shine in his mind as the ceiling fades out to reveal a moonlit night and the stars in all their glory.

God says, "You looking down at your yearbook made me travel to the sound of your heart to the rhythm of the name Evangeline. Ev-*angel*-ine. I *listen* to people's hearts, Adam. People send me to the places they want with their thoughts. Your heartbeat to the sound of her name like a drum beat in my ear reminding me of the music of the spheres the metaphysical poets wrote about, a sound similar to Saturn's gaseous hiss, projected me toward her place."

CHAPTER 2

God says, "Now there, I gaze inside Evangeline's home down another block. The shower head in a pink-tiled bathroom is turned on. Water spurts out onto Evangeline, now sixteen, grown into the girl next-door, her white bakery work uniform piled high onto the floor like whipped cream from her after-school job. Black mascara runs like paint down her otherwise innocent-looking face, and her cheekbones beautifully melt into her nose like the bone structure of a lamb. She grabs a light-green bottle of shampoo waiting on the tub floor, uncaps it, and sticks her nose into the spout. The smell of apples waft into her face like an apple pie from an oven. She closes her eyes and inhales deeply. She washes her hair."

Evangeline is staring at herself naked in her vanity mirror. Like Venus on the half shell to me, no known vanity, no known shame, exactly the way it should be for her in her room.

God says, "When the human evolved from the Cro-Magnon's animal-like kingdom to Homo Erectus's Homo sapiens, you inherited the intelligent mind that I have, which blew life into your 'id' like a glass-blown ornament. It was like putting words inside the animal's mouth in George Orwell's *Animal Farm*, and people recorded it. I may have created you, but your will is your own. *You must learn your self-made errors, which could never have come from me, to evolve from them.* And never make these errors again. *Why?*"

He continues, "For instance, tell me where it is written that I require clothes? It sometimes seems like now that you have consciousness, awareness, you don't quite know what to do with it. *Evolve.* I don't require clothes, I require your thoughts and handle *clothes or no clothes* with no difference. *Equality*. With intelligence and respect. *Evolve*. You were made to love, *not to violate*. To be or not to be better than wrong."

Adam says, "Michaelangelo, Da Vinci, the Pope, Buddha, Christ, rabbis, Krishna, Hubbard, the Beatles, Madonna—you name it, they all understand that. When did this human-made version of modesty that was laughed at in Arthur Miller's *The Crucible* become the standard for being, or incite wars for that matter?"

Adam stares at the girl at the end of the bleachers with the lotus tattoo on her shoulder. She looks beautiful to him as the smile on her face grows to the action on the field below.

Adam asks, "I wonder if we can fix that error, *evolve* again?"

God replies, "Look at your thumb. It's not a riddle, Adam, it's a *science*. It is only a matter of time until the *brain* follows."

Adam smiles nostalgically and says, "*The Panda's Thumb*, I remember well. Stephen Hawking was a genius."

God says, "It's like our sense of smell. Strong enough to smell one being in a whole crowd but we did not improve it, we *devolved* it." He looks around the coliseum and says, "but we don't really talk about it that way, do we? Sometimes we *devolve* when we let our senses go. For instance everyone here can smell the players down on the field just a little all the way up here. *Miraculous*. Don't forget that. The question becomes when you learn to be accurate, not make errors, build on love, what can you do next? *What happens next?*"

Adam looks at the girl with the tattoo. She smiles back at him. He wonders about her smell. He thinks, what if I knew that in all of New York State, I could smell her before she arrived here based on how beautiful he thinks she is. *Hard to believe!* If that's the case, he wonders, if I let her leave the stadium, for instance, without saying hello, would I still feel her energy as far away as home because of my attraction to her smell? God was right, why forget what we are or where we evolved from? *Miraculous*. And if that's the case, experimenting is just not for me, I should *definitely* get her number and be more *evolved*.

Done contemplating the beautiful woman, Adam continues, "I hope we do end the errors that *violate* what we are. Build love. End error. Grow.

Evolve." Adam pauses. "What happened next anyway with Evangeline that night?"

God responds, "Well, Evangeline is getting ready for a date. She looks down at an old photo of herself at twelve years old with you, Adam, also twelve years old, on her vanity. In the photo she is in a ballerina's leotard and you're in that childhood baseball uniform. You are smiling at each other. Do you remember when that photo was taken?"

Adam says, "Yes. It was the day of my ball game." Adam recalls Evangeline's waving hand at his childhood baseball game. Grinning, he swears he could smell her through the sweat of the players that day, he was so in love with her. "Her mother took the photo. She was a conservative woman. 'Evangeline you look like a fool asking that boy for a photo,' I remember her saying, but she was wrong. We were *best friends.*"

God says, "Evangeline, looking at the photo that night in her room, loved it. She grinned at it, fingered the image of the ballerina costume knowing she'll never trade it in for her bakery uniform; it's a dream her mother will never support. Then she goes back to getting ready for her date. Freedom came hard to her Adam. *Oppression*, genetically inherited thanks to self-made rules enforced by the adults around her. *Errors*. Rules I never came up with."

Evangeline's mirrored vanity is made of white Formica and is lined neatly with rows of lipsticks, eyeshadows, and blushes in an array of bright colors like the rainbow. Her room has changed since childhood from Crayola crayons to the berries and minerals from the earth found in her makeup that she uses to color herself in like a color-by-numbers painting. No longer do her fingers color the pictures in coloring books. Instead her unadorned face waits in contemplation for colors that after added make her look like a peacock from a children's book.

God continues, "As Evangeline stares at herself at a time when girls might want to be treated equal to boys, she is not quite sure who she is yet nor what women before her have experienced, but she has inherited a consciousness for relationships in addition to gender discrimination, *making for a difficult time*. In science all xy and xx chromosomes are first xy. The xy remains xy in some, but in others the xy continues to grow from xy to xx. The addition of the extra tail on the y chromosome when it becomes an x is the uterus—in all other ways they are the same. This means all beings are first xy and either way are all carried in an xx being whether they remain an xy chromosome or continue to grow into an xx chromosome. As such, clearly all humans, whether they are xy or xx, *know* both xy and xx genders *fully* in gestation. Separating genders is in fact *inaccurate*; they are *one* whether they remain *the same or change*. Post birth some men prefer to continue to grow to the xx chromosome and some women seek to cease growth to an xx chromosome and revert back to the xy chromosome and it makes perfect sense. The xy state is a state you must all universally become in science for a moment in time while gestating universally in an xx being, *miraculous.* Oneness. Nature. Science. *Equality*. Like the Whitney Houston song, 'One Moment in Time.'

"She scans her face and sees something feminine. Not male, different. She thinks about her gender and discrimi-NATION. Look at the word. *People don't look up their words enough*, she thinks. I think she is right, I don't think they look up their science enough either and words are science.

"She glances at her dictionary on the floor and picks it up. She turns the pages to the letter *D*. Her finger like a seeking missile scans the page from top to bottom till she stops on the word discrimi-NATION. She lingers on the parts of the word. The prefix *dis*, roots *crim-i-na*, and suffix *tion* and is scared; she sees DIS like '*to dis someone*,' CRIMINAL, and NATION. She reads the definition:

dis·crim·i·na·tion
dəˌskriməˈnāSH(ə)n/
noun
noun: **discrimination**; plural noun: **discriminations**
1. The unjust or prejudicial treatment of different categories of people or things, especially on the grounds of race, age, or sex.
'victims of racial discrimination'
Synonyms: prejudice, bias, bigotry, intolerance, narrow-mindedness, unfairness, inequity, favoritism, one-sidedness, partisanship

More:
sexism, chauvinism, misogyny, racism, racialism, anti-Semitism, hetero-sexism, ageism, classism, casteism
Historical: apartheid
'racial discrimination'

"She pauses on the word 'historical,' and says 'What a cultural inheritance. To *inherit hate, what a prison*. What a *fate*,' and she whispers 'free will, truth, a cause of action toward *accuracy* is the cure to discrimination.'"

Antonyms: impartiality
2. Psychology
The ability to distinguish between different stimuli.
3. Electronics
The selection of a signal having a required characteristic, such as frequency or amplitude, by means of a discriminator that rejects all unwanted signals.

"She thinks about computers and repeats, 'rejects all unwanted signals,' well I can at least do that to all acts of *discrimination*, then, thank you very much Webster dictionary for that definition. I am hardly interested in 'impartiality' after reading this."

God continues, "I whisper back to Evangeline, 'Never let *ignorance* rule you. Always hold a happy nature. Never let fiction dictate life. You're an evolutionary beauty. *Rejecting discrimination is right*. All humans are 99.9 percent identical in their DNA, the Human Genome proves it. All of that science and hard work that goes into making your face, eyes, ears, nose, mouth, arms, hands, legs, feet, skin, hair, and body regardless of color, gender, quantity, usability, shape, or texture is not even *appreciated* when you discriminate. What makes you unique is only worth 0.01 percent of what I see when I look at you all side by side. Most people's 0.01 percent is taken up on shapes of fingers, shapes of feet, hair color, usability of an extremity, or whether you have two at all . . . such small differences . . . *minute actually; how could you hate that either?* What your

99.9 percent is made up of is what *matters*, it takes the whole time in gestation to build. The other 0.01 percent takes no time at all, it's as long as a quick shuffle of a deck and comes from your parents only. The 99.9 percent is not only what all human beings have in common, it is hugely what the definition of being a human *is. Discrimination only rejects your own human science.* No truth is ever to be found in your world's history of "racial discrimination." One world, one human science.

"In reality the Human Genome can in one second like a nuclear explosion destroy any and all arguments around the world that claim *racism* should exist. When you look back in human history, it becomes terrifying that people could commit genocide for money. Who could do that to capitalism? Money is a neutral thing and should be a human thing that's shared, never stolen through murder.

"Knowing what makes up your 99.9 percent and your 0.01 percent should only help you share; it should never be used for you to *discriminate*. For instance, the only difference between you and a man is a uterus. Your uterus is scientific and shareable. Genders are both halves of a whole. So much so that you got it *right* in the world when you learned to share these parts with same-sex families and surrogates making sense of my science. Helping others is love. *Reject the untrue data of discrimination outlined correctly in the Webster dictionary*. What remains will be your community and *love*. Why would anyone ruin *love* with any kind of discrimination? One day the future will *sound* better, I *guarantee* it. In a future where the *sounds* in the world are better words and true scientific facts, the hate you currently *inherited* will be eliminated. If an MP3 player has the ability to compress files, billions of them, and the nuclear bomb has the ability to erase billions of people in seconds, then *positive speech and true science have the ability to eliminate forever war on topics not debatable. I guarantee it.* False communications interfere with our understanding of the universe and our place in it. Properly define it like the pages of your Webster dictionary. Enough with the *errors*."

And she closes the book.

"You know, Adam, it was like I was preparing her for what was about to come in her life. *Oppression*. Look, I created equals. People shouldn't test that. The whole world talks about me and there are still *10 percent* who have never even read my books cover to cover. I wonder if they've ever read a dictionary cover to cover."

Adam says, "It's like not including the number zero in the number line. Imagine if we had never fixed that mistake, I wonder what it would have cost us? What do our current mistakes cost us? Maybe it's like the John Lennon songs "Let It Be" and "Imagine," definitely *peace*."

God, "I think you are right. What do you think is the result of not thinking I exist?"

"That is a hard question," Adam replies.

God says, "Really? I think it's easy. For instance, these errors that lead to *discrimination* are no accident, you know, Adam. How people read, write, understand, and communicate is still being developed, evolving, and it shows. Identifying that your communication skills still need work is true. Electricity, for instance, when people say there is a blackout, they say there is 'no electricity,' but honestly, is that true? If these ballpark lights go out, is it really true that there is no electricity?"

Adam responds, "No."

God says, "We just don't speak about the universe or each other properly and we have a responsibility to stop false communication. You shouldn't be ashamed that there are errors but happy to discover them and know the difference. Like you said, it's simply adding the number zero to the number line. You have to acknowledge an *empirical fact*. For example, 'plumbing' is a human-made system, but 'electricity' is not a human development, it's a divine science. Electricity exists whether you harness it or not, the same way I exist whether you harness me or not. I am not human-made either. Whether you speak to me or not, I exist. I exist with or without religion. With or without acknowledgement from others. Religious practice does not bring me into existence any more than harnessing electricity brings it into existence. Electricity, like me, always exists. It's an empirical fact. I, God, am an empirical fact.

"So we should speak more accurately about the things in the universe that have the property of an empirical fact, which means it exists.

"When something exists, for example, we need to say it does and then describe its length of existence, whether it is capable of *extinction* or capable of *infinity*. If a fact is capable of infinity, we usually are required to educate on it, like adding the zero to the number line. *Infinity* needs to be talked about more as a concept. Without it we do not have a proper understanding of *reality*.

"Millions of things exist that we have yet to discover. When we admit that, our understanding of *reality* grows. That is *evolution*. What remains to be discovered is even *infinite*. Much of which remains to be known can continue to cure *errors*. I *guarantee* it.

"So, when a blackout happens, you shouldn't say 'there is no electricity,' that's not even true. Say instead 'there is no harnessed electricity,' a blackout. When you start to speak more accurately you evolve.

"So believing in me is a lot like adding the zero to the number line. *Accuracy*. As with the zero, I do not become extinct but am infinitely existing. That's an *empirical fact*.

"Atheism is impossible mathematically as a formula. To be atheist you must essentially remove the zero from the number line. *Inaccurate*. You certainly don't have to pick a religion, but maybe you have to say I exist *agnostically* to be correct. Being correct is the only way to have no errors. Knowing there is error remaining in science, *reality*, you have to make an effort to fix it. It's the only way to see what happens next."

Adam replies, "Einstein said the more I study science, the more I understand God. If you created science, that makes perfect sense. It's probably really hard to understand science if you don't include the fact that you exist. Kind of like working with a number line without zero. Science pushes the *truth* out and corrects errors; science has a funny way of insisting on *truth* in a way that helps people learn how to *know*."

God says, "Okay, so if electricity is always, how does it push the truth out? What does it lead to learn?"

Adam replies, "The human being cannot be born without electricity like Frankenstein in Mary Shelley's book. People are a part of electricity, it holds you together. It's what your molecules are made of."

God replies, "That is beautiful, Adam. So just add water and breath, like wind, to electricity and like a windmill of energy you are something *I made*. You are water and electrically charged energy married together in a place where it does not cause a short-out. Quite a paradox, *miraculous*. What does knowing that make you know about me? When you think about something like that, how can you talk to it? Now think about me as the maker of electricity and as electricity itself. Omnipresent, infinite. Always. Imagine if you could harness me. What would that *discovery* be? Maybe this will help you all answer the question I often hear you asking, 'What am I?' Well, you are interconnected to all things, electricity, miraculous science, part of me. Energy."

Adam says, "Even though our bodies die out like a battery? You don't die out like that and neither does your electricity."

God replies, "Death does not always eliminate things that exist. Infinity. Death should never be used as an excuse not to *discover* new information, discourage, be a distraction, or cause indifference. Death only eliminates you born *now*, your body *now*, but *not* your electricity. It continues to exist just as in a blackout. It does not eliminate *infinity* and what infinity *needs*."

Adam says, "I guess the idea of death is that it makes us miss people most and that is often all we think about. Distraction. People ask why bother to *discover*? Why not become *indifferent*? Have fun only right? Instead, if death could bring us closer to love, closer to infinity and what it needs, what people need even though we are gone, that would be better. Would that cure the problems Evangeline inherited? Her inherited fate, the prison? I wish she could have had that, but please, continue about Evangeline. What did happen next?"

God tenderly says, "Understood. The rest of that night, Adam, unfolded fairly quickly for her. Evangeline, still wearing a huge bathrobe bundled around her face, begins to color it in with makeup. She picks up a tube of black mascara and leans into the mirror carefully running the brush over her lashes several times. She brushes her cheeks with blush, and last but not least, she picks up a tube of hot-pink lipstick and very carefully colors in her lips. Done, she sits back in her chair satisfied and smiles at her reflection. Any trace of her innocent androgynous face has been painted away. Looking in the mirror, Evangeline takes a deep breath, stares deeply into her eyes, and exhales, 'Here we go. . . .' She stands up and walks out of the room to get dressed for her date, and I care very much about what happens to her next. Just like you.

"Her DNA is like a computer program to me, the color of beautiful."

God continues, "Evangeline's mother sits at the dinner table. Evangeline walks in ready to leave. Her mother is working on the bills for the month. She dons a bun and a button-up blouse with the top button done all the way to her chin. She glances up to see Evangeline in hot pink and makeup. She says to her without looking up from her paperwork, as if on autopilot, 'Don't throw yourself at that boy tonight and look like a fool,' as Evangeline puts on her jacket and slings her purse on her shoulder.

"Embarrassed, the blood rises to Evangeline's cheeks, like a cast-iron pot turning to red.

She is still a virgin and has no one to talk to but you, Adam, her *best friend*."

Adam replies, "She was a virgin? All those years? Do you know what people were *saying* about her?" He shakes his head. Tears come to his eyes. He turns to look at the game on the field below to lighten the blow. The second baseman, holding his mitt to the dirt, waits for a ground ball to call out the runner rounding first base. The score board remains 0-1 home.

God places a hand on Adam's shoulder and says, "Her mother advises her, takes good care of her, but does not *listen*. Evangeline thinks, *why is my mother talking to me this way?* She wonders, *what kind of childhood could I have if you speak to me like this? When will this end? Why can't my mother tell me I'm a nice person?* She looks up at her mother and snidely reminds her, 'I'm still a *virgin*, you know, but maybe I shouldn't be if you're going to treat me like that.'

"Her mother collects herself, brushes a piece of hair back that became undone, corrects her posture, touches the top button of her blouse making sure every button is in its place, and reaches to shove a ten-dollar bill out for Evangeline who, deflated, says, 'Thanks, Mom,' and takes the bill before exiting to the honk of a horn from the date who has arrived outside. Their relationship is thin. *The first thing you need to do in any successful relationship is be able to admit when you are wrong*. Evangeline's mother just won't do that, and it must be confusing to a child when any adult, let alone a parent, is not mature enough to admit when they are wrong. It is *correct* to simply apologize and move into a healthier relationship built on respect."

Moments later Evangeline is outside her stucco Tudor home on a wide street lined with perfectly trimmed hedges and street lights radiating with electric light harnessed for all to see best at night. No longer is the moon bright enough to light the way, even if George Bailey from *It's a Wonderful Life* lassoed it to bring it closer.

God says, "Evangeline is picked up by her date in a large sedan. I send rain and thunder to rumble in the background. Lightning cracks the darkness apart and the electricity flows in the air."

Adam says, "Rain and thunder?"

God replies, "Nothing is an *accident*, Adam. There is no chaos theory. The energy was high between Evangeline and Jay that night on their date. The kids were fine in their battery-operated tin-can cars, where their raging energy roars as they stumble like bees around the honey pot busy with their 'Paradise by the Dashboard Light' like the Meat Loaf song."

Adam lets go of the questions of errors, distractions, death, and infinity. He listens to God describe that night between Evangeline and Jay, and it is like watching Barry Bonds hit his record-breaking home run on the big screen all over again. It's like a broadcast of what went down. Jay the high school quarterback and Evangeline. The night everyone in high school had talked about all those years ago.

Adam, taking pause, glances at the woman with the lotus tattoo and wonders what her name is and whether he should ask her before the end of the game.

God says, "Now in a car with Jay, the seventeen-year-old senior star quarterback, in the driver's seat, Evangeline wears a plunging cashmere neckline and tight jeans, and her hot-pink lips are still perfectly painted on. The adult energy swelled. Jay has one too many buttons undone on his shirt, revealing a small gold football charm on his necklace, and one too many canned beers line the car floor. *Danger*."

The teenagers are driving toward Lovers' Alley, a make-out point where rows of cars are parked side by side, like the shingles of a tin roof, and bare headlights shine bright out onto the moonlit view.

God says, "They arrive at Lovers' Alley, and Evangeline and Jay park the large, unstylish car, which is his mom's. The windows of the other vehicles parked nearby are steamed up. The mating ritual has clearly begun to the sound of my thunder in the background. No *accidents*.

"Jay makes a pass and places his arm around Evangeline's shoulder. Evangeline leans in and gives Jay a warm approving kiss on the lips. The two kids begin kissing passionately. Jay, while making out, trying to be seductive, sticks his nose in Evangeline's blond curly hair, panting. 'Your hair,' breathing it in, 'it smells like peaches.' Unlike T. S. Eliot's 'Prufrock,' Jay is trying to eat the peach. He is definitely aiming to score a touchdown.

"Evangeline, ending the kiss, pulling away, says, 'Apple. It's apple.' She looks at Jay like he is a liar. Jay, recovering, says, 'Apple, right, that's what I meant. Your hair smells like apples—Granny Smith.' Evangeline, needing to pause, changing the mood, sits back against the leather bucket seats and plays with the radio, 'What are we doing here, Jay?'

"Annoyed, he looks at her and says, 'Nothing. What do you mean?' Evangeline, truthful, admits, 'I'm nervous,' while she fumbles with the stations.

"Jay, dumbfounded, asks, 'What's there to be nervous about? Come on,' as he reaches for her face, 'this is Lovers' Alley.' Silently, the two begin kissing again, speaking through their panting breath.

"Evangeline questions, 'But what will happen tomorrow?'

"Jay, frustrated, responds, 'Nothing. Nothing's gonna happen tomorrow. What are you worried about?'

"Evangeline replies, 'I don't know. Everything is going to be *different*.'

"Jay persists, '*Different?*' He continues, unyielding. 'Nothing's gonna *change*. Is that what you're worried about—*change*?' He strokes her face, locking eyes with her.

"Evangeline hesitates. 'No.'

"Jay pushes for an answer. 'Then what? What are you thinking?' The energy becomes tense.

"Evangeline feels pressured and replies, 'I don't know. I've never done this.'

"Jay leans over, touching Evangeline's hand, and kisses her, trying to put her at ease, but then aggressively grabs her breast.

"Evangeline is frantic as she slaps his hand away. 'Wait!'

"Jay says curtly, 'What? What is it?'

"Evangeline makes up an excuse. 'I, I think I heard something outside.'

"Jay doesn't relent. 'There's nothing outside.'

"Evangeline says sheepishly, 'Are you sure?' She looks out the windshield as the maple leaves fall from the trees on the glass, obscuring the dark night sky outside."

The season turns from gold to old with winter on its way, and calmer energies now settle in.

"Jay says to Evangeline, 'Of course I'm sure. And besides, I locked the doors. You're safe with me.'

"Evangeline, searching his mesmerizing eyes like a hypnotist, senses her tides turn as Nirvana's 'All Apologies' plays on the radio. 'You'll always be with me, right Jay?'

"Jay comforts her. 'Of course. You know how I feel about it. You're my girl, Evangeline.'"

Adam is still tearing up. "You know when I was a kid and a girl said she loved me and got hot and heavy about love, it didn't necessarily make me want to have sex. And being told I was loved as a way of convincing me to have sex wasn't right either. But telling the truth about my body was important to me. Saying I do or I don't want to have sex was important to me too; with or without love as a factor. My body is not a trash can. No one should have to have love to have sex. But no one should lie about love to have sex either. *Just tell the truth and be with whom you want.* So, is Jay telling the truth? This is awful if he isn't, just awful."

God replies, "Adam, she stares back at the windshield and sees one maple leaf, the tree sap helping it stick, and as it begins to run down the glass, she contemplates what to think. *Whether they are telling each other the truth only I could know* and your question is good. Without any words, Evangeline turns away from the leaf as the rain I sent outside begins to fall.

"My eyes pan through the front windshield and down at all the other vehicles parked in Lovers' Alley, getting drenched by the storm, in love with love, in love with lust, they are all seeking and finding. Seeking and finding. It feels like a flood will come and carry their cars away like arks, two-by-two."

Adam responds, "Lust or love? Who cares, either is correct. Treat one another with *respect*, right? Like the Aretha Franklin song 'R-E-S-P-E-C-T.'"

God says, "Exactly. It's not a riddle. It's a *science*."

Adam says, "For instance, I read this textbook entitled *Mass Media Ethics* by J. Christian and in it he wrote about the Agape Principle. That is, if I asked every person who reported to kindergarten class to bring a bottle of water and then instructed them to hand the bottle of water they brought to the person sitting to their right, would there be any one person without? No. This is ancient tribalism. It is the stock market. *Dividends.* It is the route to taking appropriate care of one another. It is what kids today need to learn about sex or otherwise.

"In our school, what happened the next day to Evangeline was the opposite. That's not what went down with her. *Oppression.* I mean, animals have sex to procreate, but we're *not* animals; we have intercourse for all the beautiful reasons that exist for us, and procreation is not the *only* reason. We have sex for *enjoyment*. For *education*. For *communication*. For *friendship*. For *love*. So why lie about that? In the end, convincing someone that it's for love is not necessary, and looking for love is not necessary, when it finds you and you find it reflected back at you, then it exists. Just like electricity. We don't make it. It just is. In the meantime agape sex is the right thing, that or abstaining from it if you can't bring the bottle of water. Your choice. Free will.

"And that night I had no idea where she was, but my heart skipped beats to the rhythm of her name. Ev-angel-ine. Ev-angel-ine. Not Jay's. I was actually in love with her so I know what I am talking about. But she chose him, and that night changed her life *forever*. And I couldn't change that for her. Not even as her *best friend*."

Adam rattled, "Now look, sex is not love and love is not sex, but sex is sex and love is love and sometimes sex and love come together but sometimes it comes apart. Like the Beatles song 'Come Together.' This is science. Marriage is a whole different thing. But we all know that sex is not marriage and sometimes love does not lead to a marriage. But what happened to Evangeline because of this date was a problem. No one should have their lives changed for the worse because of love, sex, or judgment about either. I mean, think of the Agape Principle. I still till this day don't know if they even went all the way. But somehow, somewhere the world said they *did.* Was it really all *gossip*?"

Trembling, Adam looks at God.

God smiles, "*Imagine* if it wasn't true?"

Adam, shaking his head, says, "I don't even want to know. That next day in school people made a choice to make a bad conversation last *forever. They* decided what went down in the car that night. Not her."

A ball has gone into the outfield and the crowd cheers as players are rounding toward home, one-two-three just like that, the other side scores. The score board reads 3-3 like two half links of a DNA chain on each side. A tie.

The girl with the lotus tattoo and Adam turn to smile at each other as they both acknowledge the run and each other at last. They *communicate.*

CHAPTER 3

Adam continues talking to God. "That same night of Lovers' Alley was different for me. I remember my small kitchen, colored yellow appliances and a long wooden craftsman style table for six. There is a plate of food neatly waiting for me at the table. I stare at it in contempt and walk over to the food pantry. My mother's cooking is from a box and it's about to taste like a paper cut to me. I open the slatted door to the pantry and eyeball the canned Spams lining the shelf and think to myself, *Why don't they make a food that has everything you need in it in a bottle so you don't have to cook at all and can leave other options for your time?*

"My mother, Susan, watches my every move as I walk around the kitchen. Disinterested in the pantry, I turn toward the table to see her already sitting there smoking a cigarette over her dinner plate and groan in my chest.

"There are four empty chairs at the table and I sit down two away from her and settle in to gobble the box-prepared meal as quickly as humanly possible and then exit hoping not to talk. Plus if I eat fast, I can play Madden video games on the TV before my dad gets home and takes over the living room.

"Staring at me she comments, 'I called you fifteen minutes ago.'

"Lying, I say, 'I didn't hear you.' I feel like I'm in *The Diary of Anne Frank* and have to defend myself against the enemy.

"Unappreciative of my words, my mother tells me, 'I came in your room and told you supper was ready.' She really was a ghost in the house.

"'I didn't know that,' I lied."

Susan stares at him. "She wonders why I lie to her. She is incapable of grasping the straws of reality."

Adam continues, "I remain silent. All she was to me as a child is an *illusion* now. The 'parent' I believed she was didn't exist. In my most secret thoughts, she is not a 'parent' to me, her own life so flawed she is still learning. I no longer can see her through my toddler eyes as my 'hero,' which she once was when I had a mind that could not understand her as more than my 'mommy.' She was like a superhero to me. I used to envision her in a costume with a cape. My mom could *do* anything. My mom *knew* everything. Then one day I saw her *lie* to a neighborhood about the truth and the Technicolor costume disappeared. She was *flawed.*

"They say the greatest disappointment for children is the day they grow up to see their parents for the *flawed* characters they are. It's like finding out Santa Claus or the Easter Bunny is not real, and for many it is painful. Some kids are luckier than I was, but tonight I was not only aware that my childhood fantasy is broken, I was behaving like it, even if my mom is still unaware of that fact. *Reality.*"

God says, "Have you ever wondered what the significance of your 'parental fate' is? Your parents dictate where you live, what school you go to, what food you eat, and the list goes on and on. How that happened to you is no more than science—the sperm and the egg. That *reality* actually dictates your life, but it also *pushes* you to use your *free will,* doesn't it? If nothing needs to change, then great. If it does need to change, you make that happen. *Your free will works inside your fate.* The onus to do or not to do is on you and you alone.

"Who your parents are is like a computer. But what you choose to design in your life, in the computer, is up to you. That's using your free will.

"I want you to see yourself as an editor of *fate* and like computer language, my language is zeros and ones, learning it can help you edit *fate.* My best advice for you back then was to program away, Adam. To think about the future ahead, a time outside of this *painful* fated home you were born in. *Free will.* Speak to others, yourself, me. They will *listen.*"

Adam says, "And I did. I did not let that fate decide my future. I reached out to others. I mass-emailed them like a computer can, and it ended up a lot like the movie 'Slumdog Millionaire,' wherever I went,

I was meant to be there, meant to know all that brought me there. I'm not so torn up about my poor *parental fate*. Assimilate to or reject your habitat the psychologists say, and I was an ejector seat set on a plane—out of there."

God replies, "Nice. The computer, you know, is a good analogy for what you are. While it's a mechanical thing fixed in its capabilities like you, made from a sperm and the egg, the mechanism itself can still be used to edit with; express your free will. You can work with its zeros-and-ones language to communicate, design yourself, and show your free will all still within it.

"When we use a thing like the computer, we need to analyze what we use it for. Do you use it for social action, for instance, or only for entertainment, and what does that mean about the choices we make? How can we compare those choices with the choices we make together with the people in our lives?"

Adam says, "Well, with my parents, if you compare me to a computer, it's a lot like the decisions aimed to try to make peace. I merged my thoughts with my genetic code and spoke to them about better treatment. On the computer we are indeed merging our *free will* with *binary code language*; expressing ourselves. Twitter, Facebook, Buzzfeed, LinkedIn, TikTok—these tools are so powerful for reaching masses and unifying them. What message do I want to send with my zeros and ones? That we can with such ease is a gift. With my parents it was not as easy."

God replies, "Well, if fate makes you feel a bit programed, think of yourself as a designer in my computer and let your free *will bring you home."*

Adam says, "I left home that night because my mother's language would cut into me in a way that made it too cumbersome, and I made a new home at school.

"Falsely accusing, she started in on me before I left. 'I came into your room. Maybe you wouldn't forget if you weren't listening to those fucking headphones all the time,' she said. 'You're always listening to those fucking headphones—they're so goddamn loud, I could be dying down here and nobody would know it. I work hard to prepare a well-cooked meal for you. The least you could do is come down on time.'

"After several minutes of silence, she suddenly breaks into tears. This sight is all too familiar to me. *Insanity.*

"She is *addicted* to talking about her problems without ever changing them. She lives for these chats with me, but it's not really enough to fix anything. We need professional help.

"She looks at me like a replacement for a friend or to keep the baby inside her womb. She cannot see me as a separate person in front of her. It's a mistake many parents make. Treating their offspring more like a possession than like an audience they gave birth to."

God says, "Do parents ever ask themselves, *what do my children see in me?* Do parents see their children as the person they leave the world to inherit? To leave a wasteland behind for your children with your tracks on it doesn't make any sense, like T. S. Eliot's *The Wasteland.* If you considered your kids *borrowed* for a time, how would you see them differently?"

Adam replies, "I tried to pry my mother open to make a difference, to get a little more information, to tip her scales. I knew she couldn't stand being with my father. The things he said bothered her. I would tell her to leave him. She was hopeless to listen but rather liked repeating herself day in, day out like a broken record for the fifteen years they were married.

"'I can't leave him,' she would say, 'what am I supposed to do? What will people think? Where will we live? We certainly couldn't afford this house.' *Distractions.* How unhealthy.

"She worried too much about rumors, like the ones about to hurt Evangeline, but I worried about the *truth.* I would assure her. 'I will take care of you, Ma, if we moved out together as a family,' but nothing worked.

God says, "She is her own worst enemy. Worried more about money than her family's health to live in a condition so sad. To value the dollar before the soul. Even if concerned for her children's well-being, really, it will always take a village to raise a family, Adam, agape, whether parents live together or apart and worse to allow gossip of the day or what other people whisper about to be the concern. *Distractions.* People's opinions can be a dangerous thing."

Adam says, "I wonder if she had just paid attention, if she knew how it affected me, what would she have done differently?

"She used to tell me, 'You're all I got. You. You're it. Don't ever leave me, Adam, don't let me be alone.' It was *pressure*.

"'You know, me and your father don't even have sex anymore? I can't remember the last time.' I was disgusted, only sixteen years old. 'I don't wanna hear this!' I'd say.

"She'd plead, 'But I have no one else to talk to, Adam,' as she places her hand on my knee and realizes she is no longer the parent in the room. 'I don't care,' I say. 'Talk to a shrink, for God's sake, not me,' and I shove her hand off my knee to leave the room. To this day I wish she had gone to a shrink.

"She snidely commented, 'We can't afford a shrink.'

"I look at her like she is made of glass, see right through her. It's like a hamster wheel where her brain should be and the words are always the same, 'I can't.' I say, 'I'm done' and move to leave the house. Game over. I was ready to *design* myself out of their lives.

"However, Mom wasn't ready for my new *program*. She followed after me onto the lawn. 'Where are you going?' she screamed, afraid. She didn't recognize this type of action. I tell her like a third strike up at bat, 'Out.'

"Relentless, she follows me, screaming, trying to gain control over my 'play' and block me. 'But I wasn't finished. You don't care. Just like your father says, you don't care about me. I put up with all this shit for you! What about me! Huh? What about me!' It's obvious she has lost her lifeline.

"I am horrified at her priorities at this point. 'What about you?' When will this design include me at all?

"She loses all rational thought and says, 'That's right, when do I get a break?'

"Biting, I state my observation, 'Ma, you've been on a break for life,' and I left her standing on the front lawn.

"Now like a nemesis from a video game, she screams after me as I get in my car, 'What, what can't you talk about?' She wants the game to never end.

"I shudder at the sound of her voice. I tilt my head back toward her, frustrated, and stare at her in silence. Knowing it all falls on deaf ears. I prepare to drive into *reality*.

"As with a nemesis, she continues her stronghold. 'Yeah, well, people make mistakes. I sacrificed my life for you. I gave you everything. If anyone's to blame it's *you*, not me. I would have left him years ago if I didn't have you.'

"I was disgusted and repulsed by her words, 'People aren't supposed to sacrifice or be in pain, you're not Christ. What heresy. You're supposed to use your actions not imprison yourself. Change.' I started my car, which I bought with my own money working at the A&P, and drove away from her *game*. I tilt my head up to look at her from the driver's seat with an intent to finish this, 'I'm not your *possession*, Ma.' My lifeline fills up with energy.

"She screamed after the car, 'You're still *my* baby. No one can ever take that from me. You're mine,' she says while shoving her thumb into her chest. 'I raised you, not your father, and I think I did a pretty damn good job!'

"I slam on the brakes and head in reverse, now eye-to-eye again. I felt as if all the stars in the sky on the day I was born must have ceased having heat, causing time to end, making change impossible. I could not live here anymore. *Danger.*

"I tell her, 'I have more respect at this point for Dad than I do you. At least he has an excuse—he's just an angry asshole who got messed up in a war. But you—you have no excuse. Why is your conversation with me instead of *professionals*? After all of these years? Dad wouldn't stop you if you tried to leave. In fact, it's probably what he wants. You're your own fault, Ma. Nobody else. Your choices. It's your greed that's causing all of the misery you see, and you're gonna die a sad, lonely woman for it but not *alone* and that's all you care about, Ma. Really odd since we all die alone anyway. Seems an awful waste of a life to live just to secure a space in the "I didn't die alone" club. I'd rather live the truth and die alone than be like you,' and I close the car door to own my fate.

"Susan looks down at me through the driver's-side window, but I drive away. In the rearview mirror her image trails across, framed by the branchless, leafless winter trees behind her, the leaves having shed to the ground were blown only by the wind from my car, and the tree branches encircle her head like skeletons around a grave.

"She turned like a zombie and headed into the house. I knew what she would do next: she would reach for a cigarette, put it to her lips, and light it. The fumes would rise up over her head like Dante's Inferno. She'd open the fridge, grab the container of Florida orange juice, slam it on the counter, and bend over into a kitchen cabinet next to the stove where she quietly stored a bottle of generic vodka. In a tall glass with a straw she'd prepare a screwdriver. She'd sit down at her plate of food with her cigarette resting in the ashtray, her screwdriver filled to the brim at her right hand, pick up her fork, and begin forking food into her mouth as she'd speak no more. Disturbing no more universe now than necessary with the sound of her voice. Sitting in silence. *Alone.*

"Her DNA like a computer virus of misery to me."

God says, "This was your home, your parents, all the men in your family, their past patriarchal place of authority is exactly what your dad became disgruntled about, the culture they created with money. Being fiscally responsible at the stake of having a dependent gender and then lambasting the gender for being dependent became a *violent* way of life for them. This inherited home was bankrupt morally and fiscally."

"Adam replies, "They were better apart. Some people should just tell the truth and have the conversation. *Divorce.* Instead there was nothing but silence on the topic.

"As I drove toward school, tears ran down my face like a waterfall forming in the brim of my eyes till they pool and flow over. In my mind, like a desert I see no future before me but tiny grains of sand sifting through my hands and years upon years and I am still here. I drive toward school resolved to sleep in the concrete jungle parking lot till morning.

"I smear away the tears and snot from my face. I pop in a cassette of me and my new best friend, Maria. She is an older woman, already graduated from high school and living with her parents, who won't support her taking off a semester from college to form a band to see where her music would take her. An out-of-my-league woman, she began working at thirteen years old and told me she would have a law degree to improve the state of her gender, write a novel, sing on tour with a band, be a film producer, and own a blue BMW before she turned forty. She was working on it all the way home. Every day. Loudly. She lived *out loud.*

"She said Michael, our four-eyed drummer, was ideal for our band because he loved house, hip-hop, electronica, his purple suede suit, and all dance music. He was perfect for drumming. He was more than bass, he was rhythm, even though he was deaf in one ear. He would play with his one good ear turned toward the drum kit, and in a funny way we think his deafness made him an even better drummer because he could perhaps *feel* the beat.

"Maria loved Edgar Allen Poe, and as a lyricist it showed. She wrote me this song that talked about parents:"

Clear across the land.
Moms and dads in chairs.
Sit and feel the sand,
sift right through their hands.
And when the smoke clears.
The water turns to tears.
And years and years.
And years upon years,
and we're still here.
Can time stand still,
as we all kill each other off one by one
and you try to look into the sun?

The lyrics make Adam cry more. He looks at the field below. The other team has the bases loaded. Yankees pitcher Andy Pettitte has to get a strikeout to avoid at least one home run. He's looking for a sign from the catcher. The crowd is silent.

God points out, "Bases loaded."

Adam says, "The lyrics made me think about *violence* and *war.* The kids in school. The street gangs. The school shootings. The buzz of all that during our generation. School violence was crazy on the rise. People were calling for a return to censorship out of fear. Tipper Gore's days of calling for censorship of lyrics by Two Live Crew and Ozzy Osbourne being sued were struck down at last by the Supreme Court, and our freedom of speech became critical. But then students were getting killed on campus in colleges and I thought *Why would you do that?* Then there were kids attacking kids on high school campuses and I thought *Why would you do that?* Maria felt so deeply about the times she was living in the same way I did and wrote about it." Adam pauses.

Adam continues, "I had even looked it up and found this list of high school shootings, elementary school shootings, and college shootings that proved violence was on the rise in the country, and this was all before 1992. It brought Maria and me closer together, as new best friends. We looked at the list over and over, it was hard to believe.

Warning: Contains Explicit Material

1960s

Date	Location	Deaths	Injuries	Description
February 2, 1980	Hartford City, Indiana	3	0	44-year-old school principal Leonard Redden killed teachers Harriett Robson and Minnie McFerran inside their classrooms at William Reed School. Redden then fled to a wooded area where he killed himself.
March 30, 1960	Alice, Texas	1	0	14-year-old Donna Dvorak brought a target pistol to Dubose Junior High School and fatally shot 15-year-old Bobby Whitford, in their 9th-grade science class. Dvorak believed Whitford posed a threat to one of her girlfriends.

Date	Location	Deaths	Injuries	Description
June 7, 1960	Blaine, Minnesota	2	0	41-year-old mail carrier Lester Betts confronted 33-year-old principal Carson Hammond in his Blaine Elementary School office and shot him dead with a 12-gauge shotgun.
January 4, 1961	Delmont, South Dakota	1	0	Donald Kurtz, a 17-year-old senior at Delmont High School, was fatally wounded by a .22 caliber bullet from a rifle. The shot, intended as a sound effect for a school play, hit him in the chest during a rehearsal just minutes before the play was to take place.
October 17, 1961	Denver, Colorado	1	1	14-year-old Tennyson Beard got into an argument with 15-year-old William Hachmeister at Morey Junior High School and wounded him. Another shot fatally struck 14-year-old Deborah Faith Humphrey.
April 27, 1966	Bay Shore, New York	1	0	48-year-old teacher John S. Lane was fatally wounded when he tried to stop 16-year-old student James Arthur Frampton. The youth was walking through the halls of Bay Shore Senior High School with a shotgun, searching for boys whom he had argued with earlier that day. Lane died about six weeks later of his wounds.

Date	Location	Deaths	Injuries	Description
August 1, 1966	Austin, Texas	17	31	University of Texas massacre: 25-year-old engineering student Charles Whitman, got onto the observation deck at the University of Texas-Austin, from where he killed 17 people and wounded 31 during a 96-minute shooting rampage. He had earlier murdered his wife and mother at their homes. It was the deadliest shooting on a U.S. college campus until the Virginia Tech shooting in 2007.
October 5, 1966	Grand Rapids, Minnesota	1	1	Grand Rapids High School student 15-year-old David Black killed school administrator Forrest Willey and seriously wounded fellow student 14-year-old Kevin Roth.
November 12, 1966	Mesa, Arizona	5	2	18-year-old Bob Smith took seven people hostage at Rose-Mar College of Beauty and ordered them to lie down in a circle. He shot each in the head. Four women and a 3-year-old girl died, a woman and a baby were injured but survived. Police arrested Smith, who reportedly admired mass murderers Richard Speck and Charles Whitman.
May 3, 1967	Northlake, Illinois	1	1	18-year-old dropout Michael Pisarski killed his former girlfriend, 17-year-old Christine Mitchell, inside West Leyden High School. The school's athletic director was wounded.

Date	Location	Deaths	Injuries	Description
January 30, 1968	Miami, Florida	1	0	16-year-old Blanche Ward killed fellow student 16-year-old Linda Lipscomb at Miami Jackson High School. According to Ward, she was threatened with a razor by Lipscomb during an argument over a fountain pen, and in the ensuing struggle the gun went off.
February 8, 1968	Orangeburg, South Carolina	3	27	In the days leading up to February 8, 1968, about 200 mostly student civil rights protesters gathered on the campus of South Carolina State University to protest the continued racial segregation of the All Star Bowling Lane after passage in 1964 of federal legislation prohibiting such action. That night, students started a bonfire. As police attempted to put out the fire, an officer was struck and injured by an object. Police later said they believed they were under attack by small-weapons fire. The officers fired into the crowd, killing 18-year-old Samuel Hammond Jr., 17-year-old Delano Herman Middleton, and 19-year-old Henry Ezekial Smith, and wounding 27 others.
March 25, 1968	High Point, North Carolina	1	0	15-year-old David Lee Walker was killed just outside Central High School by 15-year-old Gerald Locklear.

Date	Location	Deaths	Injuries	Description
May 22, 1968	Miami, Florida	0	2	Ernest Lee Grissom, a 15-year-old student at Drew Junior High School, seriously wounded a teacher and a 13-year-old student after he had been reprimanded for bad behavior.
January 17, 1969	Los Angeles, California	2	0	Alprentice Carter and John Huggins, two student members of the Black Panther Party, were fatally shot during a student meeting inside Campbell Hall at the University of California, Los Angeles. Reportedly there was disagreement over who would control the school's African American Studies Center. The shooter, Claude Hubert, was never found; three other men were later arrested in connection with the shooting.
January 23, 1969	Washington, D.C.	1	0	45-year-old Cardozo Senior High School assistant principal Herman Clifford was killed in the school's hallway by 18-year-old Ronald Joyner while trying to stop him and two other youths who had robbed the school's bank.
May 13, 1969	Winston-Salem, North Carolina	1	0	13-year-old Ernest Napoleon Carter Jr. was accidentally killed by a 13-year-old classmate at Hanes Junior High School who was armed with a pistol. The shooter was charged with involuntary manslaughter. Carter's mother filed a lawsuit against the Winston-Salem / Forsyth County Board of Education for $50,000 in damages.

Date	Location	Deaths	Injuries	Description
November 19, 1969	Tomah, Wisconsin	1	0	46-year-old Martin Mogensen, principal of Tomah Junior High School, was killed in his office by a 14-year-old boy.

1970s

Date	Location	Deaths	Injuries	Description
January 5, 1970	Washington, D.C.	1	1	15-year-old Tyrone Perry was killed at Hine Junior High School.
February 11, 1970	Philadelphia, Pennsylvania	2	1	University of Pennsylvania professors 40-year-old Walter Koppelman and 45-year-old Oscar Goldman were shot by 33-year-old disgruntled graduate student Robert Cantor during a seminar. Cantor then took his own life. Koppelman died March 5 from his injuries, but Goldman recovered.
May 4, 1970	Kent, Ohio	4	9	Kent State shootings: During protests of the Vietnam War at Kent State University, armed National Guard soldiers opened fire on unarmed students, killing four people.
May 15, 1970	Jackson, Mississippi	2	12	Jackson State killings: Two students were killed and 12 others injured when police opened fire on students gathered to protest the U.S. military presence in Cambodia.

Date	Location	Deaths	Injuries	Description
November 20, 1970	Chicago, Illinois	0	2	Two students were shot while standing in a second-floor hallway of Harlan High School. 15-year-old Kenneth House was shot in the lower left abdomen, his condition was described as serious. 14-year-old Portia Walls suffered a superficial wound on her lower back. The incident was thought to have involved gang recruiting in the school.
February 2, 1971	Philadelphia, Pennsylvania	1	0	56-year-old teacher Samson L. Freedman was killed as he left Morris E. Leeds School by 14-year-old student Kevin Simmons. Freedman had suspended Simmons earlier in the day for cursing in the hallway.
November 11, 1971	Spokane, Washington	2	4	21-year-old former MIT student Larry J. Harmon, armed with a rifle, killed 68-year-old caretaker Hilary Kunzon, who came upon him wrecking St. Aloysius Roman Catholic Church, then fled onto the campus of Gonzaga University, where he wounded four more people before police officers killed him. Harmon was described by his father as a religious fanatic claiming to have visions.
February 26, 1973	Richmond, Virginia	1	0	17-year-old Wayne Phillips was killed when he was caught between two youths who were fighting in the hallway of Armstrong High School.

Date	Location	Deaths	Injuries	Description
November 6, 1973	Oakland, California	1	1	School superintendent Marcus Foster was killed and his assistant Robert Blackburn was wounded when members of the Symbionese Liberation Army opened fire on them as they exited a school board meeting. Two members of the SLA were later arrested and convicted of the crime. Both were sentenced to life in prison without the possibility of parole. The SLA had reportedly believed that Foster supported a measure to install police on school grounds and make students carry identification cards. In reality, Foster opposed both measures.
January 17, 1974	Chicago, Illinois	1	0	52-year-old elementary school principal Rudolph Jezek Jr. was killed in his office by 14-year-old Steven Guy, a former student said to be angry about being transferred to a social adjustment center.
March 22, 1974	Brownstown, Indiana	1	0	48-year-old Jessie Blevins, athletic director at Brownstown Central High School, was fatally shot in the school parking lot by a 17-year-old student. He gave the police no motive.

Date	Location	Deaths	Injuries	Description
October 4, 1974	Kent, Ohio	0	1	19-year-old McKeesport student Ray D. Gilmore was wounded in a scuffle with two men in his third-floor campus dormitory room. 26-year-old Benjamin F. Goodman and 22-year-old Carl Bell, who were not students, had their .32 caliber pistols taken and were wrestled to the floor by other students.
December 30, 1974	Olean, New York	3	11	During a 2 ½-hour siege, 18-year-old honor student Anthony Barbaro, the best on his rifle team, killed three adults in and around his high school and wounded 11 other persons. He shot from the windows out at the street and neighborhood. The school was closed for the Christmas holiday.
February 24, 1975	Penns Grove, New Jersey	1	1	24-year-old David Gary killed 33-year-old Reverend Thomas Quinlan inside a classroom at St. James School. Quinlan was the school's principal. A teacher was also wounded.
March 18, 1975	St. Louis, Missouri	1	0	16-year-old Stephen Goods, a bystander, was killed during a fight between other teens. Three youths were convicted for the homicide.
September 11, 1975	Oklahoma City, Oklahoma	1	5	Student James Briggs killed fellow student Randy Truitt at Grant High School and wounded several others.

Date	Location	Deaths	Injuries	Description
February 12, 1976	Detroit, Michigan	0	5	Intruders entered Murray-Wright High School, shooting and wounding five students after an apparent dispute over a girlfriend of one of the intruders.
July 12, 1976	Fullerton, California	7	2	The gunman, 37-year-old Edward Charles Allaway, was a custodian at the California State University, Fullerton library. Allaway killed seven people and wounded two others in the library's first-floor lobby and at the building's Instructional Media Center (IMC), located in the basement.
November 10, 1976	Detroit, Michigan	1	0	46-year-old Al Lewis killed his estranged wife, 46-year-old Betty McCaster, as she was teaching 36 6- and 7-year-old students at Burt Elementary School.
April 7, 1977	Whitharral, Texas	1	0	High school principal M. O. Tripp was killed on the front steps of the school by 17-year-old student Ricardo Lopez for unknown reasons.
November 19, 1977	Washington, DC	0	2	"As about 50 horrified students scattered for safety, a young man wearing a hood and surgical mask yesterday shot and seriously injured the business manager of St. John's College High School in northwest Washington during a robbery attempt in the school cafeteria, District police said."

Date	Location	Deaths	Injuries	Description
January 11, 1978	Hopkinsville, Kentucky	0	1	At 8:10 a.m., 13-year-old student Andre Davis was wounded while watching a fight between two students in the front lobby of Christian County Middle School, one of whom had a gun. A 16-year-old was charged with the assault.
February 9, 1978	St. Albans, West Virginia	1	0	14-year-old Hayes Junior High School student Stuart Wayne Perrock killed 14-year-old schoolmate Arthur Clinton Smith.
February 22, 1978	Lansing, Michigan	1	1	After being taunted for his beliefs, 15-year-old Roger Needham, self-proclaimed Nazi, killed one student and wounded a second with a pistol at Everett High School.
April 26, 1978	Dallas, Texas	1	0	38-year-old Woodrow Porter, a janitor at Paul Dunbar Elementary School, was killed by the 56-year-old grandmother of an 8-year-old who was allegedly spanked by Porter earlier.
May 18, 1978	Austin, Texas	1	0	13-year-old John Daniel Christian, son of Lyndon B. Johnson's former press secretary George Christian, killed his English teacher, 29-year-old Wilbur Grayson, with his father's rifle in front of approximately 30 classmates at Murchison Junior High School. Christian was arrested and charged but not prosecuted; he was committed to a mental hospital where he was treated for a period and released.

Date	Location	Deaths	Injuries	Description
October 17, 1978	University City, Missouri	0	4	18-year-old Larry Ward and two companions were escorted from the halls of University City High School following a fight with 18-year-old student Carl Triplett. Ward ran back into the building with a gun and fired shots into a group, critically injuring Triplett in the chest and hip, and wounding 17-year-old Angela Darden and 16-year-old Jennifer Pride. Ward sustained a head injury as he was tackled by assistant principal Franklin McCallie. His companions grabbed the gun and fled.
October 17, 1978	Lanett, Alabama	1	0	13-year-old Robin Robinson was paddled by Lanett Junior High School principal Lewis Hoggs after having a disagreement with another student. Robinson left the school, returned with a .22-caliber handgun, and shot Hoggs, grazing the top of his head. Robinson was arrested two hours later about two blocks from the school and later charged in juvenile court.
January 29, 1979	San Diego, California	2	9	16-year-old Brenda Spencer opened fire on Grover Cleveland Elementary School from her home across the street, killing two adults and wounding nine people.

Date	Location	Deaths	Injuries	Description
April 16, 1979	Milwaukee, Wisconsin	0	1	17-year-old Timothy Stahle was critically wounded in the leg and upper thigh with shotgun pellets as he threw rocks at the windows of Wisconsin Lutheran High School. 28-year-old school janitor Kenneth B. Stein was arrested.
September 28, 1979	Charlestown, Massachusetts	0	1	15-year-old sophomore Darryl Williams was shot in the neck by a sniper during the half-time interval while standing with teammates and the coach in the end zone of the Charlestown High School football field. The player for the predominantly black Jamaica Plain High School team was left paralyzed. 17-year-old white youths Joseph Nardone and Stephen McGonagle were charged with the racially motivated shooting and received ten-year sentences.

1980s

Date	Location	Deaths	Injuries	Description
January 7, 1980	Stamps, Arkansas	1	0	16-year-old Evan Hampton, freshman student at Stamps High School, waited in a classroom for 19-year-old student Mike Sanders, whom he immediately killed. Hampton went to the principal's office, turned in the gun, and waited for his arrest by police.

Date	Location	Deaths	Injuries	Description
March 20, 1980	Dallas, Texas	1	0	49-year-old fifth-grade teacher Rosie Pearson was shot to death in J. Leslie Patton School by an unknown assailant.
March 26, 1980	Big Rapids, Michigan	1	0	Business professor Robert Brauer was killed in class by his 20-year-old student Thomas Kakonis at Ferris State College; Kakonis had failed an exam in his class. Kakonis was the son of an associate dean at the college.
October 31, 1980	Hueytown, Alabama	1	1	17-year-old Rudy Farmer pulled out a .22 caliber pistol and wounded a fellow student in the art room of Hueytown High School. He then turned his gun on himself.
January 27, 1981	Fayetteville, Arkansas	1	1	19-year-old former freshman James Howard Taylor brought a 12-gauge single-shot shotgun into the Delta Delta Delta sorority house on the University of Arkansas campus. He entered the house at 5:45 p.m. and terrorized an initiation dinner. After attempting to negotiate a surrender, he was shot by police when he aimed his shotgun into the dining room.

Date	Location	Deaths	Injuries	Description
April 17, 1981	Ann Arbor, Michigan	2	0	As students fled their rooms after a homemade firebomb set a minor blaze in the sixth-floor hallway of Bursley Hall dormitory, 22-year-old psychology student Leo E. Kelly Jr. fired a sawed-off 12-gauge shotgun at his University of Michigan schoolmates at point-blank range. 19-year-old pre-medical student Edward Siwik and 21-year-old resident advisor Douglas C. McGreaham died at hospitals a few hours later. Kelly had been dismissed from UM once and was on the verge of another dismissal because of falling grades. In 1982 he was convicted on two counts of first-degree murder and sentenced to life in prison.
December 16, 1981	Portland, Oregon	2	0	Shortly before noon in Engineering Hall on the school's campus in north Portland, 34-year-old University of Portland night janitor John C. Holbrook killed 37-year-old engineering teacher Brian D. Massey before taking his own life.
March 19, 1982	Las Vegas, Nevada	1	2	17-year-old Valley High School student Patrick Lizotte killed his teacher Clarence Pigott and wounded two students.

Date	Location	Deaths	Injuries	Description
April 7, 1982	Littleton, Colorado	1	0	13-year-old Deer Creek Junior High School student Scott Darwin Michael was killed by 14-year-old classmate Jason Price Rocha. Rocha was tried as an adult and sentenced to 12 years in prison, plus one year of parole.
November 12, 1982	Jackson, Mississippi	2	0	18-year-old school dropout James Hartzog killed his girlfriend, 17-year-old Faye Williams, in her algebra class at Wingfield High School. Hartzog then took his own life.
January 20, 1983	St. Louis County, Missouri	2	1	Eighth-grade Parkway South Middle School student David F. Lawler entered a study hall classroom and opened fire, killing 15-year-old Randall Koger and injuring 15-year-old Greg Saffo. Lawler then took his own life.
May 16, 1983	Dallas, Texas	1	0	Billy Conn Gardner, a friend of a food-service worker's husband, robbed the Lake Highlands High School cafeteria manager at gunpoint as she was counting the day's revenue in the office. Gardner shot her and took $1,600. He was later arrested, convicted, and sentenced to death for the crime.
February 24, 1984	Los Angeles, California	2	12	Tyrone Mitchell killed two people and wounded 12 others when shooting at students leaving 49th Street Elementary School.

Date	Location	Deaths	Injuries	Description
April 20, 1984	Detroit, Michigan	1	0	13-year-old Kelly Crittendon was accidentally killed by two classmates in a classroom at the Precious Blood School.
May 17, 1984	Pleasant Hill, Iowa	2	0	17-year-old student Todd Dunahoo killed 16-year-old Valerie Rockafellow in the hallway at Southeast Polk High School, then turned the gun on himself.
October 24, 1984	Celina, Ohio	1	0	45-year-old Shirley Shindeldecker killed school bus driver 54-year-old Gene Green as he stopped to pick up the son of Shindeldecker's estranged husband. After serving 19 months of her sentence, Shindeldecker was found innocent by reason of insanity and released.
January 21, 1985	Goddard, Kansas	1	3	Armed with a rifle and a handgun, 14-year-old James Alan Kearbey killed principal James McGee and wounded two teachers and a student at Goddard Junior High School.
October 18, 1985	Detroit, Michigan	0	6	Murray-Wright High School shooting: During half-time of the homecoming football game between Northwestern and Murray-Wright high schools, a youth opened fire with a shotgun, injuring six students with whom he had fought earlier in the day.

Date	Location	Deaths	Injuries	Description
November 27, 1985	Spanaway, Washington	3	0	14-year-old Heather Smith killed 15-year-old Gordon Pickett, who was her ex-boyfriend, and 14-year-old Christopher Ricco in the gymnasium at Spanaway Junior High School. She later took her own life.
December 3, 1985	Concord, New Hampshire	1	0	Louis Cartier, a 16-year-old dropout, entered Concord High School with a shotgun and took students 18-year-old Patrick Lena and 16-year-old Scott Hayes hostage. Responding police officers fatally shot him after he aimed at football coach Don LeBrun.
December 10, 1985	Portland, Connecticut	1	2	After being suspended for refusing to take off his hat while at school, 13-year-old student Floyd Warmsley pulled out a firearm at Portland Junior High School, shooting and wounding the 53-year-old school secretary Lynn Haddad and killing 36-year-old janitor David Bangston. The school principal was also injured while trying to escape.

Date	Location	Deaths	Injuries	Description
March 6, 1986	Dolton, Illinois	0	1	At about 9:40 a.m., as 52-year-old math teacher Norma Cooper's third-period algebra class was beginning in a second-floor classroom at Thornridge High School, she was shot in the shoulder by a freshman student with a large-caliber handgun that was registered to the youth's father, a security guard. He was charged with attempted murder, unlawful use of a weapon, and aggravated battery. The freshman, a resident of Harvey, was enrolled in the class and apparently had recently received poor grades.
April 29, 1986	Senath, Missouri	1	0	A new student, 16-year-old Ritchie Overman, killed studious 15-year-old Leslie Lynn Wyatt using a 20-gauge shotgun in front of 26 "totally horrified" science class students and teacher Sheila Adams at Senath-Hornersville High School.
May 9, 1986	Fayetteville, North Carolina	0	3	A 17-year-old student shot and wounded three classmates at Pine Forest High School with a .25-caliber handgun. One student was critically injured and treated for a neck wound.

Date	Location	Deaths	Injuries	Description
May 16, 1986	Cokeville, Wyoming	2	74	43-year-old former town marshal David Young and his 47-year-old wife, Doris Young, took 136 children and 18 adults hostage at Cokeville Elementary School. Young ended up shooting and killing his wife and himself.
December 4, 1986	Lewistown, Montana	1	3	14-year-old Kristofer Hans intended to shoot his French teacher at Fergus High School for giving him a failing grade. Instead, Henrietta Smith, who was substituting for LaVonne Simonfy, was shot in the face and died. Hans fired several other shots as he fled, wounding vice principal John Moffatt and two students. He then ran about a mile to his home, where he was arrested after the police surrounded his house. A classmate said Hans had repeatedly threatened to kill Ms. Simonfy, saying, "I'm going to blow Simonfy's head off." He was charged as an adult, convicted, and sentenced to 206 years in prison.

Date	Location	Deaths	Injuries	Description
February 4, 1987	Northridge, California	2	0	35-year-old associate professor of computer science Djamshid (Amir) Asgari was confronted in the Engineering Building of California State University, Northridge, by 25-year-old graduate student Fawwaz Abdin. Abdin was angry about a low grade Asgari had given him a year earlier, which caused him to be put on academic probation. After Asgari refused to change his grade, Abdin shot him twice, then himself. Asgari later died at the Northridge Hospital.
March 2, 1987	De Kalb, Missouri	2	0	After constant teasing about his weight, 12-year-old honor student Nathan Ferris killed 13-year-old classmate Timothy Perrin after he bullied him, then turned the gun on himself.
April 16, 1987	Detroit, Michigan	1	2	Murray-Wright High School second shooting: A ninth-grade student at Murray-Wright High School killed 17-year-old Chester Jackson, a student athlete, and wounded 17-year-old Damon Matthews and 18-year-old Tomeka Turner.
September 28, 1987	Lansing, Illinois	0	1	After being kicked off the soccer team for smoking on school grounds, 16-year-old student Illiana Christian High School student Blake Docter wounded 44-year-old John Hoogewerf, the teacher who had reported him for smoking, in the chest.

Date	Location	Deaths	Injuries	Description
December 16, 1987	Katy, Texas	1	0	After being refused a date with his classmate, 15-year-old Ramesh Guzman Tumalad shot and killed himself with a .357 Magnum revolver before 23 of his fellow freshman algebra students at Mayde Creek High School. The evening prior to the shooting, the boy discussed committing suicide to the girl after she informed school administration of his obsession with her.
February 11, 1988	Largo, Florida	1	2	15-year-old students Jason Harless and Jason McCoy took stolen .38-caliber revolvers to Pinellas Park High School. Harless shot two assistant principals and a student teacher inside the school's cafeteria. 53-year-old Richard Allen died from his injuries, while Nancy Blackwelder and intern Joseph Bloznalis were wounded.
May 20, 1988	Winnetka, Illinois	1	5	30-year-old Laurie Dann killed 8-year-old Nick Corwin inside Hubbard Woods School. Five additional students were wounded. Dann later committed suicide after taking hostages in a nearby home.
July 10, 1988	Milwaukee, Wisconsin	0	1	25-year-old Robin Jenkins was shot in the elbow after a basketball game turned violent around 7:45 p.m. at Siefert Elementary School. A 28-year-old man was taken into custody the following day.

Date	Location	Deaths	Injuries	Description
September 26, 1988	Greenwood, South Carolina	2	9	19-year-old James William Wilson entered Oakland Elementary School and started firing shots in the cafeteria. Two students and a first-grade teacher were wounded. After reloading his gun in a girls' restroom, he was confronted by physical education teacher Kat Finkbeiner, who tried to stop him; she was wounded twice. He then entered a third-grade classroom and shot toward the students, killing 8-year-olds Shequila Tawoon Bradley and Tequila Maria Thomas and wounding five others.
November 22, 1988	Abilene, Texas	0	1	16-year-old student Mason Staggs shot Cooper High School teacher Rick Maloney in the face with a pistol, severely injuring the teacher. Staggs left the school and went fishing.
December 16, 1988	Virginia Beach, Virginia	1	1	At Atlantic Shores Christian School, 16-year-old student Nicholas Elliott shot two teachers with a Mac-10 9-millimeter machine pistol, killing 41-year-old Karen Farley and critically wounding 37-year-old Sam Marino, then began firing on a classroom full of students before the gun jammed and any students were hit.

Date	Location	Deaths	Injuries	Description
January 17, 1989	Stockton, California	6	32	24-year-old Patrick Edward Purdy fatally shot five children and wounded 32 others at the Cleveland Elementary School before taking his own life. The victims were children of refugees from Southeast Asia. Purdy had a history of violence, alcoholism and drug addiction, and criminality.
February 10, 1989	Kearns, Utah	0	0	At Thomas Jefferson Junior High School, a 12-year-old boy fired a handgun at vice principal William Crumbaugh. No one was injured.
December 5, 1989	McKeesport, Pennsylvania	1	1	While riding the school bus, 16-year-old Serra Catholic High School student Robert Butler shot 16-year-old schoolmate Adam Ference in the back of the head before fatally shooting himself. Ference was in critical condition but survived.

1990s

Date	Location	Deaths	Injuries	Description
March 27, 1990	Brooklyn, New York	0	1	A black youth was taunted with racial slurs by three white youths in the stairwell of a public school in the Bensonhurst area of Brooklyn. The 14-year-old was then shot and wounded because he had acted as peacemaker when the same boys had clashed with another black teen the month before.
September 11, 1990	San Antonio, Texas	0	3	Three students were wounded when gunfire broke out at Sam Houston High School. The incident took place at 11:55 a.m. and was gang related. 17-year-old John Campbell was wounded in the right foot, 18-year-old Larry Johnson was wounded in the right thigh and calf, and a 16-year-old received a chest wound. 18-year-old Kenneth Wolford and two other male students were arrested and charged.
February 6, 1991	Donna, Texas	1	0	15-year-old Raul Calvo fatally shot himself while playing Russian roulette inside a biology classroom at Donna High School.

Date	Location	Deaths	Injuries	Description
April 23, 1991	Compton, California	1	0	A teenager aimed and fired a handgun at a security guard who had chased him and three friends off the grounds of Ralph J. Bunche Middle School. He instead killed 11-year-old Alejandro Vargas, a bystander and student at the school.
September 18, 1991	Crosby, Texas	1	0	17-year-old Arthur Jermel Jack was killed by 15-year-old LaKeeta Cadoree in the cafeteria at Crosby High School.
November 1, 1991	Iowa City, Iowa	6	1	28-year-old former graduate student Gang Lu killed four members of University of Iowa's faculty and a research student and seriously wounded another student. 47-year-old professor of physics and astronomy Christoph K. Goertz, 45-year-old associate professor of physics and astronomy Robert Alan Smith, 44-year-old chairman of the physics and astronomy department Dwight R. Nicholson, 56-year-old associate vice president for academic affairs Dr. Theresa Anne Cleary (shot in the head and died the following day), and 27-year-old research investigator in physics and astronomy Dr. Shan Linhua. 23-year-old Miya Rodolfo-Sioson, Dr. Cleary's temporary student receptionist in the grievance office, survived but was left paralyzed from the neck down. Lu then shot himself in the head and died shortly after police arrived.

Date	Location	Deaths	Injuries	Description
November 25, 1991	Brooklyn, New York	1	0	During an argument between two teens at Thomas Jefferson High School, a stray bullet killed a third, uninvolved 16-year-old student. In 1992, 14-year-old shooter Jason Bentley was sentenced to three to nine years in prison.
December 12, 1991	Kent, Ohio	1	0	51-year-old custodian John Frazier was killed outside a campus auditorium at Kent State University.
January 29, 1992	Kent, Ohio	0	1	26-year-old graduate student Sarah Smith was wounded in the chest as she was waiting for her husband to pick her up at Kent State University.
February 26, 1992	Brooklyn, New York	2	0	Thomas Jefferson High School second shooting: 15-year-old Kahlil Sumpter killed fellow students 16-year-old Tyrone Sinkler and 17-year-old Ian Moore in the school's second-floor hallway. In 1993, he was sentenced to between 6 ⅔ and twenty years in prison. He was released on parole in 1998.

Date	Location	Deaths	Injuries	Description
March 5, 1992	Obetz, Ohio	0	1	Gordon W. Dye Jr. shot his alleged bully Gregg Johnson with a .22-caliber pistol in the Hamilton Middle School cafeteria. Gregg was rushed to Children's Hospital in Columbus where doctors found the bullet and traced its path. It had entered between Gregg's eyes and traveled the nasal sinuses, where it shattered bones. Its trajectory was parallel to the bottom of the skull and was deflected by part of the skull base. This deflection sent the bullet on a downward path to the adenoids.
May 1, 1992	Olivehurst, California	4	10	Former Lindhurst High School student 20-year-old Eric Houston, killed three students and one teacher and wounded nine other students and a teacher before surrendering to police.
October 19, 1992	The Bronx, New York	0	3	Two 14-year-old girls and a 16-year-old boy were shot outside a Bronx high school.

Date	Location	Deaths	Injuries	Description
November 4, 1992	Detroit, Michigan	0	11	11 students were hit by gunfire during a four-hour period in three separate school incidents. Five were hospitalized. Six students at Finney High School were grazed by buckshot after three ski-masked gunmen opened fire in a crowded hallway. A 14-year-old was in custody for shooting three Foch Middle School students as they passed by the Marcus Garvey Academy. In the third incident, 16-year-old DeWayne Boyd was hit in the chest when shots were fired at two Mumford High School students.

"I didn't have a crystal ball, but I could see a pattern developing, and for some reason, whether the assailants were children themselves or older people targeting children in particular, schools were becoming *war zones* and no one was paying attention. *Imagine* and it only got worse, some kids went totally off their rockers, put their thoughts to action, turned violent onto one another like in William Golding's *Lord of the Flies*. In 1996 at San Diego State, a college student open fired on the campus and I wondered *Why would you do that?* In 1999 with the rebirth of the Woodstock Music Festival, people thought there would be a return to peace and love but instead, on the third day, the radio towers were torn down by the audience members and set on fire. It looked like Francis Ford Coppola's *Apocalypse Now*, and I thought *Why would you do that?* I was so ashamed of my generation. Then there were kids attacking kids on campus in 1999 in Columbine, followed by the Twin Towers terror attack in NYC in 2001, may the 2,977 lost rest in peace forever. Maria and I felt terrible about these events and continued to write about it." Adam pauses. "I really did fall in love with her."

God says, "I know, Adam, and she loved you back, but you know, in your generation the problems of your parents' generation don't exist in some ways but sometimes they do, and you inherit them. A language art of violence may have been learned in these examples and passed on somehow. Your home and these school shootings, these are homes the whole country has to fix. Communication and conversation, if we are brave enough to talk about it, can cure that. That's what Maria's song says: don't just sit there and kill each other off one by one like it's some kind of tradition, but try to make a change, try to look into the sun.

"You know, I think L. Ron Hubbard said it best that 'A civilization without insanity, without criminals and without war' is a place where honest people can prosper and honest people can have rights and freedom and rise to greater heights. So if I hear this correctly, what he said is no war or violence, tell the truth to one another, and then we can see what happens next. *Evolve.*

"Technically, the school violence needs to stop for progress in your country."

Adam says, "Maybe what Maria wrote about looking at something a new way is true. Under the issue of national security protection, these are our children, maybe we need to allow the government into our homes. Reverse camera like the big screen does here at Yankee Stadium, *live out loud like her*, then maybe we can cure crime happening in secrecy, prevent crime about to happen, and foresee who will need help in general. Conversation and communication about school violence is needed. It will take honesty and fearlessness. Truth. Sure people would scream that it sounds like George Orwell's Big Brother, but I am saying that it should be more like Dr. Seuss's *Green Eggs and Ham*. I was fearless once at that childhood baseball game, and it changed my life forever. No one should be afraid to go home. When you ask your kids to be on the forefront of a war zone while they are learning, it really becomes a humane thing to slow down and take a look at what is going down.

"Arriving at my own school that night, I left home with the last shooting only occurring one month prior in 1992. I pulled the baseball cap over my eyes and threw my heels up on the dashboard. I was listening to Maria's song on my cassette player. A hazy blue light trickled off the speedometer onto the rubber soles of my still holey sneakers projecting tiny circles of light onto my frayed jeans, which were worn out from dragging under my feet when I played ball. I switch the radio on to a ball game on the AM sports station, ending the song that was playing. I remember an orange glow from the dial.

"I think of Evangeline, my yearbook now left behind on my bed, and weep. My eyes flutter shut to the darkness of the night. The game plays on the air as the batter rounds toward first base. I was out before I heard the score and *I never went home again.*"

"For me school was now my home and if these kids today don't have a safe school these days and I went to school now, I'd have been *homeless.* Maybe they are *homeless.*"

CHAPTER 4

Adam says, "Come the morning light, the rays of the sun forced open my eyes with shards of light flickering like the blades of a fan under my lids. Blinking open, giving way from dark to light, I inhale and sit up dumbfounded to the sight of my schoolmates charging by, backpacks in an array of black and gray. I pull my baseball hat back and peer through the windshield, wiping the sand from my eyes as they land on Evangeline. Evangeline clad in a very short skirt and a rose-patterned sweater, hair out of its usual bun long and flowing into curls."

"My beautiful DNA like a computer program to me."

He continues, "My eyes dilate, letting in the physics of her energy, the calculous of her motion, the geometry of her shape. If only I were closer, my olfactory senses would inhale the formula of her smell like perfume to my nose. What a rose she was to me. A rose is a rose by any other name and its name was Evangeline."

God says, "Trigonometry, calculus, physics, algebra—these are the languages of creation. Michaelangelo only had to gaze at a mountain like the Palisades to see the *Statue of David* waiting to be carved.

"A leaf, a tree, a snowflake, Evangeline is made in this language. My language is not only found in words or human voices but in binary code."

God continues, "In the past people only understood me in words, language, and when they sought me out, they wanted to hear me in words most, like the sound of a human voice or like this conversation, but I want to ask you this: if you had to write my voice or my words down in a numeric equation like the kind you see in Evangeline, the rose, then what would it look like?

"Also, what is the numeric equation for 'Thou shalt not kill'? What would that look like? Or 'All is one' or 'Nirvana is samsara' or 'I had a dream' or 'Give peace a chance' or 'Ask not what your country can do for you—ask what you can do for your country'? I mean, JFK is talking about volunteerism, social action, love. What do these things look like?

"If you mapped words of love in binary code, what would it create? Would it look like a diamond or a solar panel? What does love of humankind look like? A baseball game? Maybe it resembles peace. A sound at a concert. A position in yoga. A lighthouse on the beach. All the universe. The miracle of a birth. Infinity."

Adam replies, "Why can't the kind of love you're talking about, the love of humankind, not permeate as the primary root of every decision in every facet of our world? In schools and homes, like you said, in government, in economy. Surely, war would become illogical and what happens next could be discovered. Progress. Prosper.

"If we didn't spend time rebuilding the past so many times, knocked out by war and violence, we could have spent time inventing things we did not have yet, but we're stuck in a bell curve. We could have built by now an electric eye that prevents anyone with a gun from coming anywhere within 500 feet of a schoolyard, or a retractable shield that can dome over the continent in the sky to block out a missile launched, or a filter at the mouth of every waterway to begin emptying the waste from the bottom, or ways to increase our chance of surviving the most common natural disasters. Where would we be in our global conversation if we had these things?"

God replies, "Makes me think about survival of the fittest taken to new heights."

Adam says, "In a world where the only thing that could make us extinct would be an unforeseeable, unresolvable natural disaster or nuclear explosion it would be."

God says, "What do you think humankind would have to use to become that kind of survivor?"

Adam replies, "Their minds."

God says, "I agree. Think with that kind of love in mind. Surely that's survival of the fittest. After all, what is the purpose of your mind if not to assist you in your eternal quest for survival for everyone? Now, *that* is winning the game."

Adam asks, "Is that everlasting life?"

God responds, "Everlasting life was homogeneously identified in so many religious languages as something that occurred in an afterlife, but yes, what if eternal life is literally here?—people's existence on earth infinitely, without extinction. Maybe it takes building a paradise, building peace, building agreement instead of war to exist, but if you did build infinity, it's out of love and gratitude. A compliment to the chef. What a nice thing to say."

Adam says, "Guess we should be good *listeners* then."

God says, "All language is divinely inspired toward the elimination of fear. Communication, this leads to peace.

"For instance, the palm of a hand raised in the air to signify 'I mean no harm' is a simple example of that principle. I speak so many languages, to be sure, I do not miss a soul for this reason. I think that's why there are so many world religions—so many dialectical interpretations, which is nice. They are all correct, whichever works for you, but they are all incorrect when they promote violence or war. They must learn to use their words. Whether the Koran, the Torah, the Bible, the Sutras, the Vedas, the Axioms, and then there is a language like physics? What are missiles built with physics saying? What are high school shootings saying?

"What do you think you should build with *science*—something to destroy, create, build, evolve, or protect?

"If Cain, the first written-about murderer, could be put into a numeric equation, would it look like antimatter? And what would the equation to eliminate him be? If Gandhi's thoughts, the thoughts of a Hindu civil rights activist, were put into a numeric equation, would it look like a mustard seed?

"We know we are the reason seismically for the hurricane, the earthquake, the avalanche, why not acknowledge it? Why not plan for it? There is no butterfly effect. There are no accidents. Build for that.

"If you permit antimatter, bombs, murder, the negative thoughts, you can only expect *extinction*, but if you do the opposite and think positive loving thoughts, your communication can cure the world.

"I can only leave you a clue about *infinity*. I want you to think about the dinosaurs while we talk. I want you to tell me everything you know about them and then compare them to humans. I'll remind you of them later, but *love*, Adam, is my most universal language—you do not need a degree for it, a lab for it, a beaker for it, a petri dish for it. It just involves *you*."

Adam says, "This conversation makes me wonder, what are the school shootings *saying*? Whether elementary schools, high schools, or colleges, these acts are *communicating* the same negative thoughts over and over, but what if *communication* of positive thoughts and acts could have saved people? First, all the places for the shootings are in schools—why? Because the targets are kids. Why? Also most of the assailants are kids. Why? The states these schools are in are different, and I don't understand what connects all of these events together to make them look like *one* mind did it when there are so many different assailants. It's not just copycatting, it's *psychological*. No matter what state you're in, being a kid today is the point. Kids are living through a hotbed of emotions. Add bullying or neglect, pressure or conceit, and the situation can become so volatile that violence can happen. At such a young age, deadly consequences may even be unalarming and the likelihood for bad expression can be high. They need *help*. Plus that's what kids see in media at large in video games, on the internet, in graphic novels, and on television. It's a part of life, but the violence in schools can be cured if the kids work together. "Parents Just Don't Understand" like the Will Smith and DJ Jazzy Jeff song is just no excuse.

"I think about my own high school experiences and negative thoughts the morning I walked into school to the *viral* rumors about Lovers' Alley, and that was before the internet or text messages existed. I can only imagine today the mass frenzies of gossip that can occur. It is completely the same kind of situation over and over no matter the generation.

"My high school was a redbrick, nondescript, industrial-strength building reinforced by metal frames, metal doors, and metal letters that read

YONKERS for those to read like a billboard from the highway passing by at a distance. The windows of the high school stare back from the building onto the world outside. The kids looking out from within, some happy to be there, others longing to be out of there into the atmosphere somewhere. Wanting the day to exhale onto the street outside to exercise, like the Beastie Boys song, their 'Right to Party.'

God replies, "Kids today are all living in a fish bowl like Pink Floyd says in the song 'Wish You Were Here.' I wonder if any of them see the water in the air? They essentially are always in a state of water. Evaporation and precipitation. They are in a *living organism*, a world that gives off toxic waste like meconium in the womb ready to suffocate you. Their language is spreading *virally* across the airwaves and the internet, using texts and Twitter, Facebook, TikTok, Buzzfeed, LinkedIn, peer-to-peer, adult-to-child, child-to-adult assault, with strikeouts on so many school campuses, a *domestic war zone*. They are already living inside a mushroom cloud, whether in their high schools or walking outside among the clouds filled with acidity and toxicity.

"They need help everywhere there is violent language."

Adam says, "Now that we know that, we need more than a Band-Aid on their schools. There have already been thirty more shootings since I graduated high school, including Columbine and Michigan. What do we do?"

God replies, "Spread the art of conversation. *Love*. Use your useful arts and science tools. Like the wheel was important to progress, you have cellular technology, radio waves, and all that connects people young and old. Use people's favorite pastimes and have conversations on Twitter, Facebook, and Buzzfeed to *spread love*."

Adam says, "In a world where government is ethical to the point of *fearlessness*, we need to turn over the reins to them, and if so, how do we work together to get money saved to spend on an endeavor like this, for communication and conversation education? For *ending violence*."

God says, "The good news is that even without temples, churches, mosques, the religions you're used to having in your home, you can still win with good, positive legal ethics in a good positive government.

You've let religions into your houses, but you've nailed the door shut to the government, and they are the ones to cure the problem. 'In God We Trust' on our dollar bill is a testament to that and it's not about any one religion. Non-salvific. Omni-loving. Omnipresent. That is your government in a democratic nation like the United States. You exercise your free will and hope that your vote communicates your dreams for the country. Your systems or veins of life such as economy, art, education, media, science, religion, capitalism, and politics must denominate a result in love for the people, and that includes your children. That is their purpose, and in that pure approach we will prosper like a spire in the sky for the whole world. Proper communication and fair systemic function should allow you to let your government in. This will help end violence. We need to climb toward progress and communicate for the benefit of the whole. If you keep destroying, your progress is limited to rebuilding and your growth is compromised."

Adam says, "Where would we have been in the absence of all our world wars? And what would we have built in that time's space? That is the question, not Shakespeare's, to be or not to be. If we permit that kind of destruction in our schools, it can only lead to our extinction. Like Einstein said, he could just look at an equation and know it was wrong.

"Then there is what they are learning in school. Can they design additions to the educational system that give them an appreciation for communication, not only the fundamentals of thought but exactly what they need to be best to one another? While you have the arts, music, literature, painting, drawing, grammar, physical and sexual education, history, geography, math and sciences, you should add organic sciences like botany, farming, gardening, orienteering, camping, home economics including making cleaning supplies, cooking and sewing, organic chemistries like pharmacological, healing, creation of perfumes and colors from scratch, cleansing, safe substance and abuse, physical movement including yoga and dance, electrical engineering, and organic and mechanical architecture, engineering, mechanics like photography and film, boating and automotives, marine biology, zoology, safety studies like fire, emergency rescue, and CPR, political sciences like negligence and foreseeability, journalism, broadcasting, psychology, pop culture anomalies including video game violence and mere advocacy of violence in media, computer design and programming, drawing and cartooning, government, the First Amendment's freedom of speech, press and religion, civic volunteerism, peacekeeping studies, comparative studies, archaeology, cartography, criminal justice, disabilities and alternative languages like brail, morse code, and sign language and help them better communicate. Just kidding—I sound a lot like Billy Joel's 'We Didn't Start the Fire'—but really some of these ideas could be added to their education if any of them sound helpful. I just wouldn't really know—clearly I'm upset—but seriously, do they even teach gender and family identity studies, ethics, war studies for prevention, recycling energies and masses, nuclear physiology, economics and fiscal responsibility as simple as *Cheaper by the Dozen* by Ernestine Gilbreth Carey, diversity studies like world cultures and world religions, the science of agnosticism, not because people need it but because it is true, foreign language studies and root word studies couldn't hurt."

God says, "Kids need support and accurate communication. You seem to think the government should do some listening. Do you think people would behave differently if they thought I was listening?"

Adam says, "I don't know, good question. You're a consciousness older than human time."

God replies, "If they did, I'd like to see that. What did happen with Evangeline in your opinion because of those rumors?"

Adam answers, "It changed her whole life in my opinion. That morning at school she walks in the room and people begin to 'buzz' with whispers about her and Jay at Lovers' Alley. She sits quickly in the seat next to me. I have 'heard' that she and Jay went 'all the way' the night before, that Jay scored.

"My pen point bursts on the page, blasting blue ink onto my fingers. I rub it into my fingertips and cover my thumb in ink. 'Damn,' looking up at Evangeline, knowing about the chatter, I whisper to her concerned, 'What the heck is going on?' Evangeline says, 'Nothing. Nothing is going on.' I tell her 'That's not what I hear.'

God says, "A curious thing Adam, you *hearing* all of these thoughts, rumors, and being concerned. Your love for her, it grows like a tree, it gives off oxygen, which feeds your lungs, the atmosphere, and other living things; oxygen becomes wind, which gives you flight."

Adam says, "That's beautiful. True. I watched over her, I thought. She cried for help, but I don't think I heard her. She said, 'Well, don't believe everything you *hear* Adam,' relying on our history as old school friends to combat the rumors but I had to know what she would never tell me. I knew I loved her but she would never be mine. 'You're with him for all the wrong reasons you know,' I told her. She snaps at the criticism, 'Don't.' She loves Jay. I pried, trying to clear the air so I could breathe, '*Why?* Why are you with him?' Evangeline doesn't respond. I pressed her, almost mocking, 'What? Are you *compelled* or something?' Evangeline pauses, leans closer to me, now sympathetic, and says, 'We're *friends*, right?'

"I lean back in my chair now that she has told me the truth. *We're 'friends' only, right?* Feeling defeated by her, I exhale a breath in frustration and stare at her without responding to her question.

"Evangeline leans in even closer despite my distance, sternly cutting the conversation to an end 'Adam, you're being *impossible*.' I don't respond. Our conversation has subsided by the beginning of class and we lost contact that day. *Forever*.

"I had not noticed, but all the students' eyes were on us while we were talking. They pan like a camera to the teacher, Ms. Michelle O. Clinton, as she walks in. She was in her sixties and had silver dreadlocks, and as she finished writing on the chalkboard and drowned out the *rumors* around the room, I still have no idea whether the couple had sex in a car the night before at Lovers' Alley.

"To put the whole thing out of my mind, I focus on the words written on the board in front of us, written in cursive. I begin to decipher the sentences like thoughts selected for me streaming into the frame of my visual consciousness. My auditory senses fade as the buzz in the room dies out as the news of the day has come to a silence in my ear drums, no more noise to the iambic pentameter of consonants and vowels in Evangeline's and Jay's names or a place called Lovers' Alley to be heard.

“I loved Ms. Clinton, she was a Howard graduate with a nose for mentorship, a third-generation granddaughter of the first African American to graduate Albany Law School and one of the first freelance internet bloggers in journalism. We loved her crazy ideas.

Ms. Clinton turns to face the class. E. E. Cummings’s poem ‘Buffalo Bill’s Defunct’ is written in its entirety on the blackboard in the shape of a *pistol* as Cummings originally wrote it:

Buffalo Bill’s
defunct
        who used to
        ride a watersmooth-silver
                                                  stallion
and break onetwothreefourfive pigeonsjustlikethat
                                                                                    Jesus
he was a handsome man
                                            and what i want to know is
how do you like your blue-eyed boy
Mister Death

“I wondered if Ms. Clinton had heard about the rumors. After seeing the poem on the chalkboard, I kind of thought that maybe she had. That maybe she was trying to help both with the idea of high school violence and the rumors. Maybe she was also saying how words can be violent too, with or without guns. That guns clearly kill but that words do too. In my opinion, that’s what happened to Evangeline, I think: she was killed by words.

“Ms. Clinton asks for the class’s attention with a voice clear as a bell. They tune their ears to her, ‘All right class, listen up. Here we go . . . turn to this poem,’ now honing their eyes into the words for the day, pointing to the chalkboard, ‘in your poetry books.’

“She takes an hourglass out of her briefcase and places it on her desk. *Time.*

“Some students hear clearly and open their books, others ignore her. J.D., one of my old childhood friends, only has his feet listen as they are propped up on his desk. Ron listens to his own tune on his Walkman, 'We Can Be Heroes' by David Bowie, as another kid, Tommy, watches the clock as the minute hand ticks by slowly like a time bomb in his unattentive, empty mind.

"Ms. Clinton, reading the poem that sounds like the *click-clack* of a horse's hoof to the class, 'Buffalo Bill's defunct,' who used to ride a watersmooth-silver stallion and break one-two-three-four-five pigeons just-like-that.' The class now hears the sound of a *time* not known to them before now. Someone's *past* is on the page. What does death and its timepiece do to a person? I stare at Ms. Clinton's hourglass and it frightens me a little that I can literally see the time coming to an end.

"My eyes look away from the words toward Evangeline. Listening to the sound of my heart most, I begin to doodle her name into the ink splattered on the page, I carve her name out into negative space. She catches my glance but quickly looks away, cheeks flushed at my stare. She really likes my attention but after a pause the blood in my cheeks dies away.

"Ms. Clinton catches the glances. She rereads a portion of the poem, 'Jesus, he was a handsome man. And what I want to know is—how do you like your blue-eyed boy Mister Death?' She pauses and looks around the room at the faces looking down at the pages.

"Ms. Clinton teaches, 'Poetry is the one literary form in comparison to novels, prose, and lyrics that has auditory purpose as well as written form. It has a rhythm forced on the ears through the selection of specific-sounding words. Words, in a pattern of sound that sometimes rhymes. The words are selected for their proper meaning and have the perfect-sounding combination of vowels and consonants. To draft a great poem, you start in a place a lot like calculus but end in algebra. Picking just the right words can last *forever*.' She glances at me and Evangeline.

"She continues, 'Also do not forget what it looks like, the shape of a gun. The author definitely wanted you to think of a gun. Any reactions to this piece? Does anybody have any idea what this poem is about after hearing it and also reading it?'

"Faced with utter silence as the students' heads sink further into their textbooks, her eyes like a camera pan the room and she stops on me, who is clearly disinterested, staring blankly at a heart and arrow carved in the ink on my page in the image of a guitar staring up into my eyes like a poem being read.

"Ms. Clinton breaks my concentration like a foghorn, 'Adam?' I look up from my carving. She asks me, 'Do you have any ideas?' Disinterested but as if my subconscious mind heard much of what was said, I answered, 'I don't know—mortality?'

"Ms. Clinton, nodding her head, says, 'Mortality?' dryly. 'Very profound, Adam.' Challenging me not to just answer placatingly, she asks, 'Now what makes you say mortality? Every word is a pregnant belly of meaning, you know.' She glances at Evangeline.

"My head snaps up in careful attention, realizing I am caught in the Socratic method of my teacher and now learn she may very well have heard about this *rumor*. I tried to explain myself. 'I don't know—'cause he's talking about death and stuff and it's in the shape of a gun.'

"Ms. Clinton continues listening and repeats my words back to me, 'Death and stuff. *Interesting*. What do you think *mortality* is?'

"I say, 'Well *mortality* is the *end of time*. To know you will die one day.' I look at her hourglass.

"Ms. Clinton, looks at me happily and smiles, 'Right, why do you think Mr. Cummings chose to speak *to* death?'

"I answer, 'To laugh at him?'

"She throws her head back, proud of my point.

"Ms. Clinton expounds, 'Death is a powerful and cathartic state to humankind, isn't it? We are all clock watching and waiting for the last grain of sand to run out of the hourglass.' She flips her hourglass timer made of wood sitting on the desk.

"She continues, 'Yet, through the rhetorical question,' she points to the words on the chalkboard, 'How do you like your blue-eyed boy now Mr. Death?' Cummings is telling death personified that he is *powerless* like you said, Adam, *to laugh at him*. Odd, since the ephemeral *death* is supposed to offer motivation in every person's life to achieve your dreams before your time runs out and so we typically want to fight that as the poet Dylan Thomas wrote, 'Rage against the dying of the light.'

"The last sand grain is about to drop into the hourglass on her desk when Ms. Clinton flips the double helix–shaped clock over again.

"She continues, 'Why is death rendered powerless in E. E. Cumming's poem? Because of the *power of language* to record the life of a person in words posthumously, this is eternal and lasts *forever*. Think of men and women like Martin Luther King, Gandhi, Rosa Parks, Ruth Bader Ginsburg, no one can erase them and their truth, not even death.'"

Adam continues, "The power of stories like the power of communication is infinite and limitless in reaching the masses, is more powerful than death. I think she is right. I wonder now is she also talking about *rumors*? Positive and *negative* speech. I hope she is. How do you kill negative speech? With positive speech. That's nothing to be indifferent about, that's what the heroes Ms. Clinton listed did. Who can help Evangeline?

"She defined *infinity* like you did too. She said 'Death should never underestimate the significance of life. That is why we have made a point of preserving stories. Your recorded history is relevant. You must always continue to preserve it and truthfully retell it as it is your dutiful love of humankind to accurately communicate.' That sounds a lot like eternity, doesn't it? Here in this poem she says Buffalo Bill has become a legend, rumored to sharp-shoot pigeons Guinness World Record fast. Whether that is true or not is up to you. I think she has *definitely* heard the rumors.

"Ms. Clinton's hourglass runs out of sand at the top. The beige crystals sit like a beach coast at the bottom waiting to be turned around to the beginning again and something tells me an hourglass is easier to restart than a person's life.

"Ms. Clinton, moving on from the topic of death in the poem continues to ask me questions about the other characters directly. 'What about Buffalo Bill and Jesus? Adam? Yes,' she paces, 'let's focus on Buffalo Bill and Jesus.'

"I say, honestly, 'I don't know. I mean Jesus could be used here as an exclamation. Like, 'Jesus, I just stubbed my toe!'

"The class laughs. Some students are still clearly disinterested, but I have Evangeline's attention from the sound of laughter in the room. Pleased, I work to make her laugh, to lighten her load.

"Ms. Clinton, playing along, says, 'Yes, that is a possibility and we will get back to him. So what about Buffalo Bill?'

"'Well, I don't know—wasn't he a cowboy or something? Didn't Kiefer Sutherland play him in the movie *Young Guns*?' I say.

"The class laughs again. I was pleased by the sound. Better than the chatter I have been listening to about Evangeline.

"The teacher, playing along, says, 'Yes, Adam, he was a cowboy. So legendary was his story that he became a performance act. By shooting pigeons, "one-two-three-four-just-like-that."' She pauses and says, 'But what has happened here, class?' The teacher looks around at them. Students are disinterested. J.D. chews gum and obnoxiously twirls it on his finger. Ron's eyelids flutter open, Walkman off, very awake.

"'What has happened to our Buffalo Bill literally?' she continues to look around at the disinterested class. 'Anyone? Anyone?' Ms. Clinton looks directly back at me, staring coldly in my eyes. 'Well he's D-E-A-D, dead, for one thing. Buffalo Bill is *de-funct*, class. He's dead!'

"Ms. Clinton disengages me and returns to speaking to the entire class. My eyes stay on her, now *listening*. 'So yes, Adam, to answer your question, *mortality* is certainly at issue here.' She turns to the others and asks, 'Anyone else? Anyone have any thoughts on this poem?'

"Evangeline jumps in, gaining interest. 'Maybe that's why he chose Jesus too then.' My heart sinks for her.

"Ms. Clinton looks back at her, tenderly smiling, and asks, 'Why's that?'

"Evangeline finishes her thoughts. 'The powerlessness of death in comparison to the *rumor* that made Buffalo Bill's legend famous—like Jesus, he won over death and lived *eternally* on the page.' I cannot believe she says the word 'rumor,' but she continues, 'People live on past death *forever*, giving the power of story and the power of a human to create a *reality*. That is pretty powerful stuff. They're all dead, like you said, but their legends have *defeated* death, have made them immortal. Death can't stomp out legends, stories are forever, and how we tell these stories, well, that just becomes the truth.' I think it's clearly what she is going through. I guess rumors can kill. Guns do too. *Death* also does but stories can give you *eternity* good or bad. The end.

"Ms. Clinton says sweetly, 'Well Evangeline, sounds like you know what we are talking about. Maybe some things are just truth and not a legend at all, it's important to know the difference. Some people *do* believe that Jesus is the son of God. So his "legend," if you can call it that, hasn't grown larger than life—maybe it just *is* life. Some things are just *true*, and not even rumors can change that. That's winning the game.' *Thank God for you, Ms. Clinton,* I think. Evangeline says, 'Thank you, Ms. Clinton.' Ms. Clinton retorts, 'No, *thank you*, Evangeline. That was *well* stated. Excellent work.' Evangeline smiles at last.

"The students now pay attention, but Evangeline looks down at her desk; she sees a heart with an arrow through it carved in blue ink on mine. Others look at Evangeline and whisper; she goes back to wishing her head would explode like in the Gregg Araki film *Nowhere*.

"I watch the minute hand of the clock tick by slowly. The class bell rings and all the students slam their books shut and get up to rush out.

"Ms. Clinton talks over the commotion, 'Please do not forget the other theme of the piece: guns. They do kill. No one but a showman should be carrying guns around. Be mindful of each other's safety. Okay, class, that'll be all. Make sure you read the next assignment. I don't want Adam and Evangeline to have to speak for all of you again tomorrow, even though maybe they *should*.' Evangeline looks up in awe. Everyone hurries out of the classroom sheepishly.

"I linger behind to wait, slowly packing my bag at my desk and hoping to talk to Evangeline. She looks at the drawing again and hurries out without acknowledging me, and that's all I ever knew from her side of the story."

God says, "Not realizing you drew the heart, Evangeline thinks whoever doodled that, *They understand me.* That's what she said before she exited the room that day without speaking to you, Adam."

Adam responds, "That's *sad.* Ms. Clinton asked me, 'Everything alright?' and I responded, dejected, 'Yes, everything's fine. Really.' Ms. Clinton said, 'Because you seemed a little lost earlier. Let me guess, some girl got you all up in a rouse?' I shrug off the suggestion. 'Nah, I don't know. Maybe, I guess.' Ms. Clinton, knowing I want to remain silent on the subject, offers this, smiling, 'Always the chase. You know, there's no better ink than the blood of a broken heart.' Looking down at my drawing in ink, I say, 'This is different.' Ms. Clinton says, 'It always is.' She turns over her hourglass and leaves the room for me to be alone to think.

"In that time she gave me, all I ended up thinking about was the night before with my mom and not going home. I thought about not going home. Not. Going. Home."

CHAPTER 5

God asks, "Did you talk to Evangeline about not going home?"

Adam replies, "No, Maria."

God says, "Tell me about Maria."

Adam explains, "Later that day in the high school cafeteria I'm sitting at a large round table like the Knights of King Arthur alone. Watching as kids stroll in for the lunch line like factory workers from Pink Floyd's *The Wall.* I see Evangeline and perk up like a percolator coffee pot but realize she is walking next to Jay. I slump back into my chair decaffeinated. The rumors were still buzzing, and I could tell everyone in the room was leaning toward them being true. So *I* started leaning that way too. . . ."

God asks, "What made you think so?"

Adam replies, "They stayed together."

God says, "But she told you. . . . Don't believe everything you hear."

Adam says, "She avoided all eye contact with me the rest of that day and walked close to Jay holding his hand. Jay sees a friend of his checking out Evangeline and high-fives him, clearly approving the ogling. I am *disgusted.* Since she began dating Jay, she had lost several friendships and I didn't know what to do. So I just thought at that moment to give up on figuring it out.

"My best friend, Maria, enters the cafeteria and rushes toward me. She is wearing combat boots, ripped jeans, and a Pearl Jam T-shirt. There is a guitar case on her back and she is carrying some papers.

"She takes my mind away from the rumors for a while and I am happy. I can think again about myself and not going home. She's excited. '*Duuuuude!* I have been looking for you everywhere!'

"My concentration on Evangeline was completely broken. Maria could do that.

"Maria realized she broke my attention and turned to see what I was looking at. Evangeline and Maria lock eyes, a knowing look because they have seen each other before. Maria sits on the table in front of me, purposefully blocking my view of Evangeline. Maria should have been a guidance counselor, but she had a funny way of letting you decide whether to hang yourself with your own rope, so I'm not sure that fit the job description. If you needed *love*, she was there for you, but if you wanted to destroy yourself, she'd have to report you to the principal and do the *walk-away*. She rolled her eyes at me and tries an assist, gesturing to the couple Jay and Evangeline. 'Awwww, c'mon dude, get over it.'

"Agitated, I look up at her and say, 'Whatever Maria, okay? What do you want?' I pause, I cut her off. 'No, wait. You don't even go to school here. What are you doing here?

"She smirks and says, 'That hurts, really. Are you saying you're not happy to see me? Seriously dum-dum, we have some work to do, and I love it when you call me Big Poppa like Biggie.' Confused, I ask, 'What work, what are you talking about?' And she hands me a flyer and says, 'Take a look.' The flyer reads:

DOBY SKY at the PYRAMID NYC
Saturday September 27, 1992
Doors open at 8 p.m.
Cover $10

"I look up at her and say, 'This is a flyer for a show, at the Pyramid, and it's in the shape of a pyramid, Maria.' She says, 'Yes. I know. I made it myself. The flyer also lists other bands in the line-up.' She is fearless."

Adam continues, "The band we formed is named Doby Sky. If you look up the word in a dictionary it reads:

Doby | Home
verb–To report (a person) to someone in authority for a wrongdoing.
verb–To do one's share; to contribute.
verb–To nominate a person, often in their absence, for an unpleasant task.
do-be
dōbē/
noun–a poet, a bard.
noun–alt. sp. a kind of clay used as a building material, typically in the form of sun-dried bricks.

"For us the band was a planet, a world unto its own. A home, and when we were there we were under its sky—she called it a poet's sky—and we were nominated to contribute stories for the world like Bob Dylan and make a change for the better. *I felt safe with her.*

"I look up at Maria again this time nervous and in disbelief. 'You booked us a gig?'

"Maria was excited as she hopped off the table. 'You're darn tootin' I did!' she said, grabbing my arm and forcing me to walk with her. 'Now let's go, we got a lot of work to do, kiddo. I wrote a new song, and we have to practice it like a million times,' she rambled, 'and this is going to be *amazing*. Are you psyched? I brought your guitar, see?' she said, pointing to her back. 'I knew I didn't have to start college yet.' She points her finger at me, squinting her eyes. Give it one year I told you, one year, Adam, and . . .'

"Cutting her off, I stop walking, afraid. 'Wait. Wait. I have classes.'

"She looks at me, exacerbated. I am clearly in her way. 'Give me a break, Adam. Really? Class? You're on lunch. Live a little.' Determined, she says, 'Let's go, we are out of here. No discussions. This is important to me. Don't be such a dork.' She pleads sweetly. 'Please.' She walks out of the cafeteria, not waiting for me to respond.'

"I stand still and see her moving quickly down the hall, laughing. She *is* fearless. I begin running to catch up with her. She didn't even notice I hadn't followed close. 'Okay, okay. I'll go. But promise me you'll drive me back before last period, okay?'

"She concedes, teasing, 'Yes, yes, just let me show you this new song at least. Then I'll drive you back to school. Okay. Geez, loosen up, will ya? How old are you now, like 50?' Laughing, we *always* laughed. 'Ha, ha. Very funny,' I quipped, 'unlike you, some of us take school very seriously.' She stops, *my soul mate*, I say in my heart. I look at her. We pause.

"She acknowledges my seriousness and we stare at each other for a moment, and then she breaks the moment. She teases me. 'Yes, Adam, you are the *mature* one.' There is sarcasm in her voice. 'You ground me for sure.'

"I say, 'Ground you? Ah, no one can ground *you*, Maria.' We laugh. We *always* laughed.

"She is so *respectful*. 'No, seriously dude, I get it.' She elbows me. 'I know you need good grades. I got your back, you know that, right? I would never mess that up for you.'

"I say, sincerely, 'Thanks.' Dead silence. I needed help. Then, teasing her, I say, 'Because if I don't get a scholarship, I'm gonna have to ask *your* parents to pay for college.'

"She smiles and rolls her eyes. 'Great. At least they'll be happy one of us is going right away.' We laugh. We *always* laughed. We turned to exit the cafeteria together. If someone told me then I wouldn't know her today, I would have punched them in the face like the Pink song 'Who Knew' says. It makes me speechless."

God says, "I know, Adam." He places a hand on his back.

Adam tears up, shakes his head in silent contemplation of the moment. "She was exactly what I needed to leave home. My *best friend*. Right on time. 'A gig, huh?' I reflected on it and told her that day, 'You are one crazy woman.' Maria responded with sarcasm, 'Thanks, love you too, Adam.' Sarcastic again, she says, 'So wild I am. Wild and free. *Sosososososo* wild.' Yet I could hear it in her voice that day, '*Not even you understand me, Adam Weakley*.' No one *really* did. A disappointment echoed in her chamber heart like the raven in Edgar Allan Poe's words, 'Nevermore, hark the Raven nevermore,' and we exited the school together *safe and sound*.

"Maria and I went to a park, where there is a footbridge. It's suspended over a piece of the Bronx River narrow enough to see its borders while looking down its center. The dew-covered leaves of golden sunlit maple, loaded beautifully, cover the planks of the bridge for passersby to slip on. We were cloaked in winter coats, hats, and gloves sitting on the footbridge passing over the tiny river in a park. She has a sheet of paper with lyrics on it and I have already begun playing my acoustic guitar, the sounds floating from its wooden hull, strumming new words in keys making the music up as she sings the new song's melody."

The lyrics:

I want to do nothing and leave this place.
Walk around naked,
at my own pace with you.
We can sit in the grass counting stars,
wondering what is out there.
Act like we're five throwing wishes to the sky and
they'll look and they'll think that we were high.
I want to do nothing with you.

God says, "That's beautiful."

Adam replies, "She was the best friend I ever had. Made me who I am today. I wondered, do I dare kiss her? I feel like a thief on a baseball field looking at her from a catcher's crouch waiting for her to throw the next ball. I stared at Maria as she sang, her eyes big and beautiful looking up toward me from time to time, like the Cyndi Lauper song 'Time After Time,' but mostly she looks down at her lyrics shyly. Her voice sounds nervous like a ship needing a buoy to guide it steadily, she'll find her voice one day, I can hear it "Break on Through" like the Doors song, and I wonder do I dare, do I dare like 'The Love Song of J. Alfred Prufrock' eat a peach? Do I kiss her? She looks up at me. I have a big grin. I am appreciating her. 'It's really, really good, Maria.' She, open to criticism, says, 'Really?' I say, 'Yeah. Totally. Beautiful.' She excitedly hugs me and says, 'Thanks Adam!' She quickly stands up, and I miss my pitch to kiss her. She hurries and says, 'Okay let's bolt.' Teasing me, she says, 'I have to get you back to school, remember?' I'm a little dazed and disappointed to go back to school. 'Uh, yeah. Yes. Thanks.' Maria responds, 'And don't worry so much about Evangeline. She'll come around,' she says, rolling her eyes, 'They always do. . . . But here we go, Adam. The Pyramiiiiiiiid. Here we go!'

"Gone to her feet, I follow her Tasmanian devil's tornado dust trail. She continues, 'We really have a load of practice to do before the show.' She turns to stare me down, 'Every weekend,' she locks eyes with me, 'promise me.' I have not told her I am not going home yet. Laughing, I say, 'I promise, I promise.' I pause then say, 'Thanks Maria, seriously, this is *awesome.*' She said, 'I know,' dead serious, 'you owe me one.'

"All our hopes and dreams were tied to the floor bed of the ocean like a beacon calling us home for this little show to go on without a hitch, and in that moment again I became a raindrop in a body of water the size of an ocean. Fearlessness set in.

"'I do owe you one,' I told her. 'Agreed.' Maria, sensing something was wrong, lightening the mood, says, 'But it *is* . . . it *is*," and she screams, '*Awesome!*' We laugh, we *always* laughed, and start to run through the park happily toward her car, hitting the bridge with our feet, not slipping on the wet leaves, and in our young hearts we created a place free of charge for our empty pockets, lined with nothing but cotton, four minutes long, a song for *free*. Creating something for free—art. It never charges you to create. To see the trees, rivers, lakes, oceans, and birds is always *free of charge.* To inspire. To create, no matter where we are. Free.

"We protected each other. We helped each other understand how to create. This was our conversation and it was *divine.* It really spoke to me. Forever. *Infinity.*"

God says, "I know exactly what you are saying. *Infinity.*"

CHAPTER 6

Adam says, "Back at school I got to the boys' locker room. It is lined with gray metal lockers, some propped open, some propped closed. Many contain baseball and football gear. It looks like something out of John Irving's *Hamburger Hill*."

He continues, "It was good to get away from the rumors and chatter for a while with Maria. But now back, as I walk farther, I hear Jay, '. . . and like that, boys, she was mine. It was paradise I tell you, in the back seat of my mother's car. A grand slam.' He pounds his fist into the palm of his hand like a baseball mitt. The boys laugh and high-five each other, celebrating his triumph like he is their hero. I stand a few lockers down from the boys, crouched over tying my Converse shoelaces. I mumble under my breath, 'You freaking *idiot*.' Is this story even *true* I ask myself.

"Jay overhears me. Looking for a distraction from his story anyway, he turns to pick a fight and deflect his audience. 'What? What did you say, *D-I-C-K*? Jay moves confidently and aggressively toward me and I realize my life is about to change. I rise to meet his stare. Jay gets up in my face, ready to fight. We look like two roosters beak to beak, chests cocked, guns loaded. I am nervous, almost terrified. Yet my disgust is overwhelming.

"After a moment of silence, I finally speak as if wanting every syllable of my words to be heard properly by Jay. 'That's what I said.' Jay, cocky, says, 'Why's that, now? What, you have a thing for her or something?' I'm surprised. I thought it was hidden. Jay, not waiting for a response, confidently turns back toward his friends and continues to show off, and ignoring me, says, 'Well there's plenty more where that came from, guys. Besides, she couldn't resist me. I mean, what can I say?'

"I, interrupting and sarcastic, challenge him and say, 'Plenty more, huh?' Jay turns to me and says, 'Yeah, that's right. There's plenty more, and if she won't do it, someone else will. She knows what she has to do to keep *me* around.'"

God says, "I was there, you know. I saw what they did, like the Phil Collins song 'In the Air Tonight.'"

Adam acknowledges, "You know the *truth*. I was still not sure. So I pressed him. 'Yeah right, what crap did you have to tell her to do it, huh? You *liar*. I suppose you told her what? You *love* her?' With my best emasculating baby voice, 'That the two of you would get married, live happily ever after, right?' Jay, slightly embarrassed by the suggestion, says, 'Hell no, *what*?' to his friends. 'Yo, check this fool out, talking about marriage. And anyway,' to me he says, 'I'm gonna marry me a virgin—and this girl wasn't no virgin, if you know what I mean.' Jay motions like he's having sex, thrusting his pelvis into the air. The other boys all laugh at his display, high-fiving each other. Fed up and enraged, I grab Jay and throw him into the locker, getting right up in his face. Shouting in Jay's face, I say, 'Well I would! I would freaking marry her in a second, if I could get rid of you and she wasn't so stupid,' loosening his grip, 'You're *pathetic*. Keep your freaking hands *off her*.' Not waiting for a response, I swiftly exit, walking right through the middle of the gathered crowd as if parting the Red Sea, pushing one of them aside.

"Jay, stunned, gathers himself, shakes off the total fear he just felt and uses the feelings I have revealed to recapture his throne. Jay, yelling after me, 'Oh look, *weakling* the *virgin* boy's in love and wants to get married. I hope your dick don't fall off, *fag*!' All laugh again. High-fives follow. Jay continued his sermon, totally unaffected. 'See what I'm saying boys? God, I love this country. You got enough virgins to marry, and enough whores to bone. Milk and honey, baby. *Milk and honey*.' The boys look at Jay in awe.

"I haven't been called *weakling* in years. Hearing the word *fag*, I turn around and go back, picking Jay up with both my hands and hurling him into a locker. 'There is nothing wrong with being gay, *nothing*. Now which am I, Jay? Gay or in love with Evangeline? Why don't you tell everyone that story *next.*' I release him, stumble back exhausted, stare at the kids. 'Don't believe him, he's a liar. Check your facts, don't be a loser like him. Just walk away.

"Jay continues, 'Boys, don't believe everything you hear.'"

The bell rings as if the main event of a boxing match has ended in a tie at the twelfth round and everyone begins to shuffle out of the locker room. Two of Jay's Friends walk out together, discussing his tale, and one friend says, "I can't believe he did it. I can't believe he *scored*, and what a fight. Who do you think won?" The second kid responds, "Neither." The first kid says, "Yeah that's true."

Whispering is heard in the hallway as students begin to retell the story of Jay's "conquest in the back seat of his mother's car" and about our fight in the locker room. It spread like wildfire. It exploded on Evangeline like a bomb and it changed her life. *Forever.*"

The school bell rang again. It's like something out of Mark Robson's *Peyton Place.*

God says, "Do you at least think you did the right thing?"

Adam says, "I don't know, not even till this day. I'll never know if I made things even worse. I wanted to protect her. I was the only one who wanted to protect her, and maybe I believed her too somewhere down deep inside when she said not to listen to everything I hear. Maybe I understood what she was puttin' down. I at least did that day. At least that minute, and I defended her."

God says, "Everything a bully ever has to say is *myth*. It is their version, a delusion, but not truth, not empirical anyway. Even if a bully is popular, what they have to say is never what the truth *really* is. The bully's *intent* is not to be heard but to hurt or control another person. Think about it, everything they say is to put themselves in a position of power. The bully isn't even concerned with what they are actually saying. They are more concerned with power than anything else. It's like something out of Machiavelli's *The Prince.*

"Murder, judgment, racism, hatred—all of these experiences are *useless.* Remember, to get rid of pain does not make us weak but makes us powerfully strong. Ideal. That's paradise. The bully can never build paradise.

The bully is never engaged in fair competition either since lying is never a characteristic of the fittest unless it's to overcome corruption. The bully is *corruption* and would never use lying for any other purpose but to empower itself and telling the truth would end its reign. The bully can never win the game. That's *ethics*.

"Again to reiterate the 'Anne Frank' example because it's *enlightenment*, if you knew lying to a soldier banging on your door would save the life of Anne Frank, who is hidden under your floorboards in a world where someone tries to tell you lying is an absolute wrong, I have to ask *why wouldn't you lie?* Wouldn't lying to save her life put you in the proper prioritization for a better world? After all, wasn't the soldier banging on your door lying in the first place to gain power? Destroying that kind of power is *enlightenment* and *paradise* can only exist without it.

"The bully makes up less than 20 percent of the population, so I guess the other 80 percent are made of the fittest love, which is the 'Greatest Love of All' like the Whitney Houston song says. Careful that you understand what you're listening to so you can stay safe and sound. Don't assume you know and don't believe everything you hear, there are a lot of *rumors* out there. Check the facts like you said, Adam. Take the time to know. Stay safe and sound.

"On Jay's assault on the same-sex nature you defended, no one should use science to belittle one another. Having sex and not having sex are both natural too. Your partners of any gender are always natural selection. It's time to listen to science. That's *enlightenment*."

Adam says, "You know, during the Reagan era, we had to teach kids about drugs to have the war on drugs. Here in high school with bullying, people should start talking more about what they hear to protect themselves from liars and use the war on drugs campaign as a format for a war on *lies* campaign. The use of communication and education to fight the lies that inflame school violence, rumors, and bullying that lead to shootings needs to be shared. Twitter, Facebook, Buzzfeed, YouTube, TikTok, and LinkedIn should be used to share what's happening in the minds of the high school peer groups. Clearly, the mind is the stomping ground connecting the states where these kids are going to school and the internet should make it possible to keep them safe and sound, not the other way around."

God says, "Listening is an art, Adam. A free one."

CHAPTER 7

Adam says, "*Listening* when people talk it is an art. I listened most to Maria when she would sing. I loved talking to her. I never went home again and I married her." Adam looks at his hand and there is no ring there.

He continues, "I remember one night the sound of thunder from a rainstorm. She had just turned thirty. Still a young, beautiful woman, but more sophisticated now. She wore cozy yoga pants and a tank top revealing an intricate rose tattoo on her spine, and was sitting Indian style on a yoga mat in the dimly lit bedroom facing incredibly large floor-to-ceiling windows. They were completely bare and reminded me of her. No curtains disturbed the breathtaking skyline view she was a part of. Her angelic eyes are closed, she is in quiet meditation, face *peaceful*, hands resting on her knees, and she wears my wedding ring. That night looked like *enlightenment* to me.

"She looks out at the New York minute and contemplates the noise pollution and light pollution that can make it hard to hear her own voice let alone my voice and her *inner* voice on some days. She would say if you go out to a more remote spot, you can hear more clearly, and she tries to find it nonetheless in Midtown Manhattan, in a 'New York State of Mind,' like the Billy Joel song, on her *inside* while surrounded by all the smog and bright lights of the bustling city below.

"In the city people flock here not to be alone, she would say, and they look up and say 'There are no stars out,' but really, as you know, there always are stars above the smog and light pollution. It's like saying there is no *electricity*. The stars, of course, are always there, but you can't always see them. 'You should drive out somewhere to take a look once in a while for a good *listen*,' she would say, like the Orb song 'Little Fluffy Clouds.'"

God asks, "Why? What's the *value* of looking at stars? In the past you used them to navigate, inspire, and to light the way.

"Does living without stars affect your quality of life? Does having them make it easier to listen to others more if you look at the stars? Is that the same when you look at a city? A building? A country? If so, what do you build in its place if it's gone or what do you do to preserve it if it's not? Maybe you should build and preserve the places and spaces where you can listen best like a river, the moon, a lake, a mountain, a field of wildflowers. 'You belong among the wildflowers,' as Tom Petty and the Heartbreakers sang, 'somewhere you feel *free*.'

"Going to a place where you can *listen* better is good after being in places and spaces where you *hear and see* nothing."

Adam says, "Maria was that *place* for me."

God says, "You're lucky you married her then."

Adam replies, "Yes. The New York skyline looks like a lotus flower in her eyes reflected in the glass pane in front of her. She, with care, had photographs of us line the walls. Images of us hiking in the rain forest, wedding in the snow, fishing on a lake, playing guitar, kissing. Mostly cheerful and candid, this is clearly a happy married couple. Several framed academic degrees on the walls including a Valedictorian Award in my name. I did it with her help, and now I'm going to rebuild the new Yankee Stadium like the Taj Mahal and preserve baseball, the American pastime, just like I had planned before I was sidetracked by that awful job down on Wall Street, like Oliver Stone's *Wall Street*.

"I remember coming home that night. I entered the room in a suit and Vineyard Vines tie with anchors on it holding a tumbler of scotch on the rocks. I see Maria silhouetted by the skyline. She looks like a sun drop of light, like a lighthouse whose ray shines like Pink Floyd's 'Shine on You Crazy Diamond.' Pivoting, I pause and smile. She is a sight for my sore eyes. I take a deep breath. I put my drink down on an end table by the bed, pull on the knot to loosen my tie like a noose slung around my neck, throw my jacket on the bed, slide my shoes and socks off with my toes, unbutton the top two buttons of my shirt, grab my drink, and quietly sit down behind Maria to join her yoga. She remains undisturbed.

"I stretched out my legs around her, take a sip of my drink, put it down next to us on the floor, and wrap my arms around her. Resting my blunt chin on her shoulder, I close my eyes. At the same time, Maria's eyes open wide and she smiles a happy *peaceful* smile. Maria softly whispers into my mouth, 'Hey Adam.' I quietly moan into her skin, 'Hey *love.*'

The yellow light of the moonlight shines down into the room glazing it like a pearl.

"Maria, nudging my chin like a hummingbird with her shoulder, says, 'Long night, huh.' I bury my nose in the sweet smell of her hair and inhale her. '*Mmmmhmm*, you could say that again.'

"Maria says, 'I like the way you inhale, did I tell you that? I like the way your hair curls around your forehead, I like the bow of your dimpled smile, and the way your chest plate looks like a turtle's shell. I like the way you breathe, I like the way your nose crinkles when you're laughing, I like the way your eyes wrinkle together and your beautiful black brows burrow into your arc-shaped eyelids." Maria places her hand behind her, where his chest has met her spine, and she rests it on the base of his neck as if it were his heart and whispers, face tilted like a boat going in at an angle to quiet a storm, now still, 'Glad you're home.' This home was filled with positive words.

"I kiss her shoulder and say, 'Me too, Maria,' as I place my hands around her hemisphere like a boat in longitude and latitude headed for her compass rose. Her flat belly rises and fills with air at the quiver of my wakeful heart's beat. Our sound is a peaceful, peaceful wake.

"Maria notices my drink and teases, 'Whatcha got there?' I playfully pick up the drink, 'What, this?' Maria, coy and seductive, says, 'A sip please?' I hold the glass up to Maria's lips as she takes a sip. When she is done taking a sip, she moves her lips to kiss my hand, she gently takes the glass from me and puts it down and begins to sweetly move toward my lips and we tenderly kiss. What is in a kiss? The kiss ends and we hug. I hug her tightly from behind again, she reciprocates hugging my arms more deeply into hers. What is in a hug? My hands move lustfully to her breasts and we kiss again. What is in my hands?

"She turns to face me on the floor and wraps her legs around me tightly. We hug again deeply and she sings. I listen. She quietly sings into my ear. 'I want to do nothing.' I look up at Maria and smile. Singing, still quietly, our childhood tune, 'And leave this place, walk around naked, at my own pace with you.' What love is in her voice, and I listen. I kiss Maria's shoulder, I plant a kiss with each note on her as my lips travel up her neck, onto her chin, teasing her mouth, onto her jaw, off to her earlobe, back toward her cheek, up to her eyelids. Her face, my favorite constellation. I warmly land on her forehead, my favorite part—where her mind is—as I cradle her face in my hands and gently rest her lips on my head.

"We both pause, a tender moment, looking deeply into each other's eyes, saying nothing, just sharing a deep loving stare. Our iris's dilate to black, letting the light come all the way in on the *inside*. The light shows our *truth*, it is the only way we see things in proper form, natural light. The space between us dissolves and our lips meet. What a conversation.

"My hands passionately pull her hips in closer toward mine, my fingers can't get her close enough to me. She slides my white button-down shirt off my shoulders and bundles it around my waist to pull me closer, like a ship coming to dock. We embrace, kiss passionately, trying to close any space between us as we melt onto the floor to make love.

"I look into her eyes again as the iris of her core opens to flood them like the arc of Noah. I float, containing life to no end, eternity, like the twelve nights of oil that kept a light ablaze on Hanukkah, like Paul Revere's last ride through our country's terrain of mountains and grains, one if by land, two if by sea for her and me to be free.

"Inside and outside. On top and under. She and I went to the sea with laryngitic human voices, in a wake of silent reverie. *Love* our morse code, *blinking. Blinking. Blink. Blinking. Blink* to carry us homeward like mercury in fixed form staring face-to-face and singing ear-to-ear, her love calculably infinity like binary code to me and no known computer program for me to speak of and it speaks to me, it speaks to me, it speaks to me. Love. So I hear her speak to me and fill me too. Like a thread through the eye of a needle end-to-end we two meet; a *circle*. Eternity."

God says, "Beautiful."

Adam says, "I have not found a *place* like Maria since. I wish I could have preserved it, but it was like the Coldplay song 'In My Place.' I couldn't."

God says, "Why not ask what can you build in its place, to honor it once existing? She had a positive effect on your quality of life and helped you listen. That is a special *place* to lose. Love."

Adam says, "I think maybe it's rebuilding this place, the stadium, for the love of the game."

CHAPTER 8

Adam says, "Can you imagine a world that is so quiet that I can hear your voice in it, God?

God replies, "Really? Once upon a time people went to work to put my lyrics down in prose in the Bible, the Torah, the Vedas, the Axioms, or the Koran. Imagine how I must have been *heard* then."

Adam pauses and says, "Perhaps like this conversation?"

God says, "Maybe Adam, but tell me," he places a hand on Adam's knee, "about your life's conversation with Maria. What did she say to you that was so positive?"

Adam replies, "Nine months after that night of yoga, our baby Francis was ready to be born. Our alarm clock rings. I wake up. Maria, practically full-term in her pregnancy, is asleep in the bed. I get up and enter the bathroom, shower, shave, and dress in a suit and tie, any one will do. I walk out of the bathroom and kiss Maria on her belly before leaving for work.

"Several days of the same routine pass him by. Life seems like a hamster wheel of threads and money, chemical smells on suits, and shiny cars, martini lunches, and business by moonlight.

"I was at work really late one night while Maria slept on the bed alone. She was editing a manuscript entitled 'The Absence of Me,' and beneath the title it read: A Novel by Maria Fresia Weakley, Fifth Draft. A red pencil is in her hand.

"The television is on, and when I call her, the sound of a baseball game can be heard, the crowd cheering as she answers my phone call. Wakeful, Maria tells me she has to grab her uneaten red apple next to phone.

"Back at the office I am sitting like a dot in a leather chair at a desk, in a room, in a building, on a street, in a city called New York. My single window is mirrored from the outside to keep the glare of the sun and heat from making my room hot. I can see the *outside* city clearly through the tinted gun-metal glass. It is busy and filled with traffic. The people below merely 'ants marching' like the Dave Matthews Band song says.

"I'm on the phone with Maria, the phone sits next to my computer, a blinking DOS cursor on the green screen and a shortwave portable radio, which is the focus of my attention. The sound of paper being shredded in the background can be heard. The radio plays the same baseball game Maria has on the television at home.

"Maria, still asleep, answers, 'Hello? Hello?' She stammers into the phone. I, softly excited, say, 'Oh sorry, did I wake you? Did you see that play?' Maria, waking up, says, 'No. No . . . I fell asleep, damn it,' she laughs. 'What happened?' I, laughing, say, 'Sorry I woke you. Nothing, never mind, you can read about it later. How's our little prince?' Maria dreamily rubs her belly. 'Oh, fine, waiting for me to eat the apple. Baby Francis is doing just fine. So what happened today?' I say, 'Francis? I thought we were going with Ben?'

"We muse a couple expecting the baby leaping and bounding like a gazelle in her womb. So excited, she was nesting and preparing. Working and loving her days ribbons and blue

like his eyes will be shore.

"Maria laughs and says, 'Well, you decided Ben, I decided Francis. Seriously, stop it. How did it go today, what happened?' I answer, 'Nothing. Nothing happened today. I'll tell you about it in the morning. Go back to sleep.' Maria, conceding, says, 'I love you,' and I say, 'I love you too.'

"Maria asks, 'Are you still waiting to hear from Don?' I answer, 'Yup, you know the drill, he's still moonlighting a client.' Maria knowingly says, 'Ah, strip club again, huh? Clown.' Maria sometimes cannot believe where the people that built New York City are forced to work. I say, 'Yup, he's such a jerk.'

"Liltingly, Maria says, 'Don't make a big deal of it. Just go, get it over with, and come home. We miss you,' she says, rubbing her belly. I say,

'I know. Okay. I love you,' always feeling better when I hear the sound of her voice. Maria replies, 'Love you too. Wake me up when you get in, okay? I want to hear all about it.'

"I laugh and say, 'Will do. Miss you.' Maria, acknowledging my tone, says, 'You know, Adam, it's all about choices. I support you, whatever you do. Money is for life not in place of life, okay? Now go build the circus.' I try to change the mood. 'I know, you go eat that apple.' Maria and I together say to each other the same words, 'Love you.'

"We both hang up. My hand on the receiver still holds the resonance of our loving voices and it lingers there, in the technology."

God asks, "What did you have before technology? What a beautiful conversation to capture. You being apart from her now you only have memory. I can't see you, I can't hear you, I can't smell you, I can't touch you, but because I have met you face to face, ear-to-ear, I can know you and recall you only in my mind before technology existed. Now with technology I can hear you and see you. What utility will memory have to us short of recalling facts on our own and those we've lost but not recorded?"

Adam says, "You are not wrong. You should record your memories with photos, videos, the internet, cameras. Build your story. Store your memory. That's a place you can build to improve your quality of life."

God says, "After Maria hung up the phone that night, she fumbled the apple to the ground watching the game."

Adam says, "I wish I had known that. I swear I wanted to get home to her that night, I was *so* impatient. At the office, I stand up, grab the redwell file off the shelf, and head for the door, paper still being shredded in the distance. I exit the room into a narrow hallway whose drop ceiling and cubicles look like a geometric pattern calculating infinite sadness.

"Now at the elevator, I can see my reflection in the steel metal doors. I look like Superman as Clark Kent, straighten my blue shiny tie in the brushed nickel, making my image look sad. The doors pop open and I slide inside and begin my dissent to the street level. I am not happy at all to be at work late on this major ball length night. Game playing is not my favorite at all, and I love my girl more than my boss knows. I think to myself 'I'm going home now instead of to Angel's strip bar and chucking this file for a Chuck E. Cheese in Brooklyn, where I hate the germs and love the noisy bells and whistles like Gertie's shriek in the play *Oklahoma*, who was hottest to me as a man on the prowl when I was a little kid in Harlem. Hot girls rock my world and Maria played Gertie when she was a kid. I am adorable and distractible while I secretly study to be the top dog on top of the film set for stories my wife writes because her mother was right and our time will be soon, I hope, for our cute baby. See how he holds us back all those years. The end. I win best writer award for knowing everything. Now go home and tell Don to go to hell.' I grin to myself. I laugh at my truthful code, I am clearly unhappy and losing it at this job. *Olololololololololololololol.*

God says, "What a moment."

Adam replies, "Wait, it gets worse."

CHAPTER 9

Adam says, "So exactly one hour later at Angel's a Gentleman's Club, sexonomics is in full swing like a Grand Old Party for a candidate campaigning in the flesh and blood, literally. 'In God We Trust' is on every dollar bill sticking out of G-strings in the line of sight from its pyramid with the eye on its back. It's an upscale club with a 'heavenly' theme. The women are dressed like angels and goddesses, wearing either wings or see-through togas. The men are well dressed, mostly in suits. Some smoke cigars, others drink expensive brandy. The girls dance topless on stages throughout the club. There is a strict zoning code here. Men and women ogling strippers sit like kings in large cushioned chairs, some with naked angels on their lap. The girls not dancing glide through the club, offering their services.

"I spy in a chair not far from the main stage Donnie 'Big Business,' who bought and sold, forgot the cry of needing, only wanting more. An ocean of things, ornaments of profit, while others drown at the shadow of his hand. Don, seventy-three years old, southern, an overweight man in a suit, sits with two younger businessmen at a table and a naked angel on his lap. He sees me enter holding a redwell file and waves me over. I roll my eyes knowing the night is going to be smoke and mirrors. Literally. Sick of it all I say, 'Here we go. . . .'

"I walk through the club hardly noticing the beautiful women dancing around me and politely turning down any offers made by them. We hear the end of a story Don was telling the younger businessmen, 'and he could sell a dildo to a nun I tell ya, just like that!' All laugh. I arrive and am greeted by Don and the other men sitting with him. We shake hands. A dishonest ritual for Don for many years. Don knows he is clearly holding them under and in his mind knows no one really wants to be there with him, but he *needs* the company.

"With his collar undone and a drink in his hand, Don rambles to me, his face flushed from drinking. I, by comparison, look pale and disgusted as I listen attentively trying to mask my contempt. Don states authoritatively, 'You see, you can't make an omelet without breaking some eggs. The *profit and loss*. Sometimes you gotta make sacrifices, lose some of the crew to keep the ship afloat, take one for the team. Hell, that's what this beautiful country was founded on—*sacrifice*.'

"He reminds me of 'Buffalo Bill,' a myth, but he has a negative effect on lives and I don't like it. A gold crucifix around Don's fat, sweaty neck—I wonder how it got here. *He is the opposite of Christ*, I thought. Probably a gift from his octo great grandfather who owned a plantation once. Crazy how anyone could use a religion to oppress, but like all miracles, that very religion was used right-back-at-ya the right way to *liberate*, like the real king, Martin Luther King, did. I thought of the *liberation* ideology of Bob Marley. I thought *'Don't Worry' Don* like the Marley song 'one day you'll be *free of telling lies*.'

"Don continues, 'That, and working harder than the next guy. Now sure, my daddy was in the business, and his daddy before him, but nobody said life was fair. You play the hand you're dealt. . . .' *Fate*. Gold and diamond rings choke Don's swollen, greasy fingers like a noose. Don continues, 'You know, spin the wheel, see where it lands.' Don will take whatever is on the table. *Glutton*. 'All men may be created equal, son, but they sure as hell weren't born equal. Hell just look at the Indians, we came here and massacred the whole lot. Turned this island into a money-making machine. So what if we had guns and they only had spears, only the strongest are gonna survive.'"

"And I couldn't have disagreed with him more. What survives? A loss? If you had to steal it, you're not strong. Only what is built without having to give it back is strong. If you steal your profit, it's weak, you have to give back. Your profit is already earmarked as a loss when the police arrive. And I couldn't have disagreed with him more.

"This man is an heir from *Kubla Khan*. The opposite of me. The convex of Leonardo DaVinci's *Vitruvian Man*. How I weep a *Valley of Tears* for the eggs and spears, the Natives and their lost tongues and fears. How now brown cow, I know *more* than him. He is *viral negative words*. I wait to meet him at his death day aboard the misspoken preamble of the Constitution. All men *are* created equal unless you're a crook, which he is. His survival, a scam. His power, corrupt. He is a weakness masked as the fittest like the bully Jay was. Alone. Just. Like. That. Liars.

"In the survival of the fittest, I wonder if his company will live a day longer in a newer world where Americans are calling for a tin-can car in their veins, that wash our rivers clean and earmark their brown sites for cancer that green their chimney stacks and light their oil drums on fire. 99to1.99to1.99to1. Till the labor law legislates a yearly 10 percent increase based on profits only realized, but they raised the minimum wage instead. I wonder if it will work.

"Don's binary code is in need of emergency resuscitation to ololololol, a game called on account of rain, back from his Vincent Ward's 'What Dreams May Come' death. Nice heroic Fatherhood Dad for my wife, but I did not long to be a business partner here. I am a real tried-and-true red, white, and blue ball game corporation, pure capitalism, pure growth, pure prosperity, pure progress, pure agape principled economics for *all to share* with care a bottle to our right one-to-one, for each neighbor to be out of poverty and in with humanity, to 'put a love to good use' from the work of Elizabeth Barrett Browning 'How do I love thee, let me count the ways.' Let's count capitalism rooted in democracy, humility, to end homelessness, end hunger, end drug addiction, end sexonomics, end unemployment, to shatter the glass ceiling for leadership, to demolish the national deficit, to treat the employee humanely, to degender the work force with equal profit for all. I was going to quit this job. I was going to rebuild the Yankee Stadium in honor of a Constitution that requires progress in the useful arts and sciences. Anything that does not is unconstitutional. I was going to give the people a useful place for both. *Art and science*."

"God says, 'Adam, at least you're the man with the plan. It sounds awful with Don. Maria home peacefully sleeping again on the bed. I know you would have rather been back at your apartment that night too. Her orbiting baby Francis in a universe in his mother's womb home. What you said is a lot like 'Right Now' by Van Halen, and I *appreciate* you. Democracy and capitalism communicating together can cure the world of poverty and pain. Build *paradise*, Adam. Build it."

Adam says, "Maria . . . I'll never forget leaving the bar that night to get back to her. The red neon lights created a fire around Don as he talked about me to hold me there. 'It's all God's intention. There's good and there's evil. There's heaven and there's hell.' If this was hell, heaven was home with Maria. He continued, 'This earth, it's all garbage headed for recycling heaven in my opinion.' He's not thinking about the world of *progress*; to him the world is a junkyard and he's just a scavenger in it. Still holding me there, he talked me up. 'And you, you did a hell of a job today, son, hell of a job. You're the real savior here. It doesn't matter about those other folks, they'll manage. And I sure am proud. So don't feel bad, boy. Just be glad you're on top of the mountain. I mean, look at this place, baby, it's paradise.' It's *not* paradise, and he's just a crook with no talent for business and he knows it. Time for me to go *home*.

Girls dressed like angels pole dancing, men still putting money in G-strings, businessmen and women being led to lap dances in back rooms. This is all Don has. *Alone*.

"That night was a total lost and found for the lonely. As if it could not get worse, Don asks a young Angel to call out the next dancer. Out walks Evangeline, no more the innocent-faced girl I knew. She walks onto the stage to ruin my life. She sees me. Our eyes lock without responding. Doing the best she can to own her a tin-can-can-car, she smiles at me and dances. I watched her dance, no ballerina leotard for her here. It made me sad since my baseball uniform *was* still with me.

"I think of Maria at *home*. I know she's fallen asleep by now, it's 3 a.m., like the KLF song '3 A.M. Eternal,' I glance at my SEIKO watch. I know back at home the television is still on, all programming has ended, and the American flag waves on the screen.

"Don is still huffing and puffing his cigar. He exhales and says, 'It's all about winning, baby, and you sure hit yourself a home run today, son, a home run.' He sits back in his seat to watch my old high school love Evangeline. Having heard enough, I say, 'I should be getting back, finish things up.' Handing Don a pen, I say, 'Can I get your signature on these to finish the deal?' Don says, 'Awww, don't worry about those, you didn't even have a drink yet, let me buy you a drink.' Cocking an eyebrow, he adds, 'Or maybe an Angel?' he grins. I, resolute, say, 'No, no, thanks, really, I'm good. Lots more work to be done you know.' Don concedes but asks me to leave the documents with him and says, 'I have to go over these with a fine-tooth comb, you know, the one you use to catch lice.' Laughing, Don grabs the pen and signs the papers anyway but *holds them back*.

"Annoyed, I shrug. 'Sure, sure. Don't work too late now, we've got a big day tomorrow.' Hearty laughter. Placating Don with false excitement. 'Gotta make this shit company look good enough to buy! That's what it's all about, right?' I tap my finger on the documents, like a man happy to play his part and go *home*. Getting up to go and leaving the papers behind, I say, 'Enjoy the rest of your evening,' and under my breath, 'We all die alone, asshole, but you'll definitely *deserve* it.'

"I think of Don, his love of money, and I think I have his number. Zero. A loss. He makes people proud to be who they are. That's his purpose. He's a *measure*. That is his number, a zero, nothing to compare to and everything to measure up against. Makes me a ten, I think. A profit.

"I walk toward the exit and swiftly cross Evangeline's path. I hear 'Oh my God, Adam,' and turn to see her breath. Evangeline, distracted by Don, turns her attention to him briefly. Don stands from his chair, raising his arms in the air, calling to me as I exit, 'Home run! Home run!' Don is pulled by a stripper back into his seat, as he laughs sinisterly.

"I do not look back as I reach the door, the mirror ball turning in the club refracts the images of the people down below in its squares. I exit. Evangeline follows in tow. I do not see her.

"Out on the New York City streets, which at this hour still feel like the office day has just come to an end for the commuting class, I exhale a huge sigh of relief outside of the club. Evangeline, barely dressed in a sheer pink mini toga with a black hoodie over her two-piece stripper wear, stands beside me now. Tears well up in her eyes, of course. I pause to see her.

"Losing balance, her platform velvet pumps make her stagger into me. Tears have turned her mascara into black streaks of makeup under her eyes and she chokes my name from her mouth, 'A-dam.' I see her a mess to behold. I look at her and wonder what to say, it's been so many years since we have seen each other. Since high school.

"She says meekly, 'Hi. Remember me?' Thrown off-guard, I say, 'Evangeline, is that you?' I look up at the 'Angel's' sign above her. Flashing, flashing, a bright white light, the word 'Angel's' is written in neon triple-lined tubed letters. I look down at her, six-inches shorter, and see she's been crying. I fumble through my pocket to hand her my handkerchief. 'How are you?' I ask. She looks up at me like a tiger with glassy eyes and red nostrils from damaged vessels and chuckles, 'How does it look?' She cocks her head to the right. She smiles to lighten the mood and *connect.* I look at her bare legs in the air and see she has barely any clothes on, 'Do you need some money? Cab fare? Are you on your way *home*?' Here, I'll hail you a cab. You should go home.'

"I step away and hurry to the corner and hail a cab. A yellow taxi pulls up. I open the door, not sure if it's for her or for me. She walks behind me, stumbles on the words to say, afraid she'll lose her *time* to speak. 'I felt good. When I was with you; understood.' The words make me cringe. I throw my head back, close my eyes, and shake my head in disappointment. Explaining myself, I tell her, 'I'm married, Evangeline, but I understand it's because you felt loved. Accepted. Supported. Encouraged. Believed. *Loved*,' I step closer to her endearingly. 'Those are good qualities and you should continue to look for them.' She takes a step closer, inhales. I step back, 'Sorry, I'm very nurturing lately like a dad. You see, Maria is pregnant so I have been reading up on parenting a lot.' I smile.

"Evangeline pauses, taking it all in. 'A baby? Wow. A mother huh? And you, a father. What do fathers do? The same thing as mothers, right? Are they taught today to do anything less? The men in my family don't cry. You start out crying the moment you are born and yet people are taught not to cry. Seems like a shame to teach you to be hard and cold like I've seen, like that. Make sure your baby sees you cry.

"'Since I was a child I would read about 'What I Am' like the Edie Brickell song. In literature too, you know?' She raises an eyebrow questioningly. 'What am I supposed to be like? It was scary. Jane Austen. Madame Bovary. Adam and Eve. Not for me. That was a *good* thing.' She begins to pace in place, rambling, hoping to make sense of herself. 'But I am not them. No rule in any book anywhere told me I had to be like them or that I broke a rule. *Disobeyed.* That makes me so happy. *Free will.* Those writers are like bullies trying to steal my natural development, but then you have to tell yourself it's just a story right?' She stops to look at him. I stare back blankly. She continues, 'And I always have a *choice* to be whatever I want, make sure you tell your kid that. Free will. Some choose to be like Cain. Why? There certainly are rules about that in books somewhere. You'll end up in prison. You know what I think Cain is for? To show *bad* thinking. He's a *measure* of what not to do. Like those rumors back when we were kids. They decided what I did, not for my benefit but for their fun and games. They were *bad* thinkers. Rumors can kill a person. Hurt your mind. I would never choose that.' She continues, 'You know you can strike my cell phone in my hand and have it considered assault on my body, but throwing your sexist or racist words at my brain is not? Because it's speech? That's not free speech. That's assault on my brain. My brain is my body.'

"I ask her, 'What are you going to choose with that free will?' She responds sternly, 'I'm still thinking about it.' I laugh. She lightens the mood, 'Hey, it feels like high school again, Adam, talking about all this literature and stuff right? Like 'Buffalo Bill' and Jesus.' The lights from the traffic signals reflect green on Evangeline's face. I stare back at Evangeline now stopped, blushing red. Having nothing to say, I bolt forward toward Evangeline and grab her tightly, hard, as if it speaks volumes to hug her. *What is in my arms?* A *brain.* I release her, look into her eyes. She says, 'Thank you, Adam,' and I say, 'I have to go. Thank you. It was nice running into you this way,' and I get into the cab. And just like that, I leave her there on the sidewalk. *Free will.*

"I slump down in the back seat and look at my hands, empty of any papers I had gone there to have signed. I was not upset but found the experience altogether livid in the afterwomb of my thoughts. I rather had spent the night with Maria listening or watching the game instead of bringing Don the papermill work force. Now in the cab, I followed up with the game and I knew again this time this night was a *lost and found* cause. Evangeline. Evangeline. By the third beat it became an afterthought on the sidewalk.

"The driver of the taxi is from India and wears a burgundy turban and a sweatshirt made of American cotton. He's a tried-and-true polite man and a happy man, and he asks his customer 'Where to, Sir?' I say, 'Home.' The driver asks, 'Where is home?' and I say, '111 2nd Avenue between 50th and 51st, please.' He says, 'Yes, Sir.'

"I look out the window into the NYC night. I see young people pass by, a couple holding hands, a lady walking her dog, the beginning of the after-after-hours after-work crowd dwindling down mingle in the traffic and building lights; they look like constellations, NYC stars fallen from the smog-filled, starless sky. The stores change as they continue uptown from the adult playland of Times Square to the high-end stores surrounding the Playboy offices, Tumi, Gucci, Escada, and the more they become high-end, the closer I get to 'home.'

"I ask, 'What's the score?' The driver responds, '4 to 3. The Yankees just got a leading run.' Enthused, I say, 'Alright. Sounds like another championship this year.' The driver agrees. 'Yes, maybe this is true.'

"I say, 'Of course. They're unstoppable.'"

"The driver responds, 'Yes, well, they have the most money.'"

"I laugh and say, 'I take it you're not a fan. What's your name?'"

"'Oh, I am a very big fan. Bashi is my name,' he replies."

"I reply, 'Really? What teams? Nice to meet you, Bashi. I'm Adam.'"

"Bashi says, 'Oh, I do not like teams, Sir. Likewise nice to meet.'"

"I say, 'But you said you're a fan.'"

"'A fan of baseball, Sir, yes. America's finest sport,' Bashi replies.

"Confused, I ask, 'But you don't like teams?'"

"Bashi says, 'No, that is correct. I do not have a favorite team. I just like to watch the game. I do not care who wins, only that there is a good game played.'"

"Understood."

"Bashi laughs and says, 'In fact, it is the winning that makes me most sad. Because when you win, the game is over. I had a mother who would talk to me about winning, but I used to tell her when all is said and done, if I *love* playing in the sunlight out in the field with my fellow friends and smelling the grass and dirt smeared on my face, then it is not the win or loss in your heart you want, it's to keep playing.'"

"I reply, 'And when you did that, you eliminated *time* and created *infinity* in a second, didn't you, Bashi? I had a teacher in high school who taught me to do that once with an hourglass.' I smile to myself."

"Bashi, pleased his rider understands him so well, says, 'And let us not forget that when there is a winner, there is always a loser too. In my way I win one, you win one, I win two, you win two, I win three, you win three, the game can go on forever.'"

"I reply, 'Sounds like the stock market, Sir.' We laugh. I see what he means, 'Yes, well, of course.'"

"Bashi continues, 'Again, I would like very much to see everybody play the game, forever. That, Sir, would be true happiness.'"

"I reply, 'What about other sports, do you like any other sports?'"

"Bashi says, 'No, not really, Sir.'"

"'Not even basketball or football? Or what about soccer?'"

"Bashi says, 'No, Sir.'"

"I say, 'Hockey?'"

"Bashi replies, 'No, Sir. I do not like any of the games you say, Sir.'"

"I continue, 'What about golf?'"

"Bashi replies, 'No, Sir. Nothing. All of the games you say must end, Sir. But that is the beauty of baseball—it can go on forever when there is no *time* limit on this game, Sir.'"

"I say, 'Unless someone is ahead after nine innings, bringing time home, because we do have a *time* limit, Bashi.'"

"I reach over across the plexiglass cab divider riddled with breathing holes and place my right hand on Bashi's shoulder, '. . . because we do all have a *time* limit, Sir.' Bashi looks briefly back at me, the customer, riding in the back of his tattered pleather-lined taxi and smiles gingerly at me. 'Right, Sir, which is why I hate to see winning and losing, Sir, because then the game must end.' He pats my hand and goes back to driving. *What is the value of winning and losing?*"

"I sit back in my seat laughing. 'Say, what's your name again? You're an intriguing man,' I say with a Cheshire cat grin, contemplating his next move homebound in the tin-can taxi cab dreamboat drive to *home*. Rooftop Penthouse in the sky."

"'Bashi. My name is Bashi. Pleased to meet you, Sir.' I say, 'You're an interesting guy, Bashi, an interesting guy.' Bashi, flattered by the thought, says, 'Thank you, Sir.'"

"The car rolls up to a tower building covered in steel and glass. A building modern and window-filled with no cement or brick. A building just like the once basement blast by the white supremist domestic terror clash survivor in 1993 and second successful attack caused by foreign terrorists hijacking domestic commercial airplanes that eliminated them in 2001. *Winning and losing*. I remember taking Maria to the Windows on the World to ask her to marry me. The only spinning restaurant in NYC. I will *never forget*. Never forget *losing* those towers. *Never forget* telling her I love her in them. On my bended knee, chest pounding, surf-and-turf, one-if-by-land-two-if-by-sea dinner set to candlelights in her eyes. She said *Yes, yes, yes,* like the Yankee Network, and made my day.

"Those towers fell dark on 9/11. Forever in our hearts in our wedding bands. Baby Francis waiting to bring us a vestige of those buildings and our life shared there back. To be born in NYC.

"I was working on September 11 in 2001 inside a building on Beaver Street for the Division of Housing and Community Renewal. I was a political appointee of Senator George Pataki there even though I was a liberal Democrat and liberal Republican, which they called an Independent then. I remember seeing Senator John McCain, the POW veteran hero, run for president in 2000 on the steps of the Stock Exchange four blocks away from the World Trade Center, where the city that never sleeps came under attack one year later in 2001.

"I *remember*, I will *never forget*, I walked down sixty flights of stairs to the street below wishing the whole way down that I knew what was happening. McCain had once said that while he was a POW the one thing he missed most was not his bed, pillow, food, or people. It was *information*. Free-flowing *information*. Once I met the street outside, I saw ashes everywhere and the sky was gone. People were covered from head to toe in dust. It was like Pompeii.

"Bodies lie on the ground, no sounds coming from them. This was a civilian place but now a war zone with no trained military in sight. The firemen and police everywhere responded like heroes. No one survived in the buildings.

"It reminded me of the footage I studied of World War II as a student at the United Nations, the mass graves, there were so many bodies in these graves. Not everyone made it to the concentration camps. There were graves where civilians lived, off roadways between villages, in the side yards and backyards of their city homes. The kind this city has in Brooklyn, Queens, Staten Island, Manhattan, or the Bronx. It was not only in the camps that these piles of bodies were found.

"In some graves people of all ages were fully clothed, others had their clothing stripped from them, then others had only skulls left by the time they were found.

"World War II was a war of terror. The enemy was hidden in plain sight in *uniform*, *uniforms*, giving the false impression of peace keepers, uniforms recognized by many to symbolize protection created the confusion and delay that caused so much death. People became confused, hypnotized by the authority of uniforms. Who knew clothes could deceive that way? Underneath them were cannibals, animals, and their insignia of skulls advertised it.

"That day he walked over the Brooklyn Bridge to get to my then *home*, a basement apartment that we rented in a single-family house in Spike Lee's Bed-Stuy. I learned what had happened on the news, despite the rumors all around during my commute with other pedestrians about bombs, but there were none.

"The news reported that two commercial planes had been flown into the neighboring skyscrapers by male passengers dressed in civilian clothing. They had taken over the cockpits and killed the pilots. David Angel, the network producer, was a passenger like the Astors on the *Titanic*. Wearing civilian clothes, no one could see this coming either, like Gordon Parks in a Gap ad, how sanctimonious. What does it mean when you hide so hard you dress like a civilian? *Winning and losing*. Who can protect us now? Aren't civilian clothes confusing?

"Maria and I watched the news for forty days before we turned it off, and we both honored the Marshall Order to remain out of the city until the clean-up was complete. Maria dropped off canned foods in boxes left out on the sidewalks for collections and was fired from her SoHo Hotel check-in desk job, as no tourists would be coming, they said and apologized.

"The heroes were down at what became coined Ground Zero. Workers from everywhere in the nation, from sea to shining sea, were there. The firefighters, police, EMS, doctors and nurses, construction workers, utility workers, volunteers, *civilians* . . . the whole nation became New Yorkers. Toni Morrison, the author of *Beloved*, wrote a poem commemorating the day by the title 'The Dead of September.' She and I had a 'mouth full of blood' like Apollo Creed and Rocky Balboa. Amiri Baraka, poet laureate for New Jersey, wrote 'Somebody Blew Up America,' asking 'who' owns America? Bush was out at bat at the next election and Obama was up at the plate. Thank you for your service. Winning and losing.

"Now in front of this *home* building fashioned and modeled after those Twin Towers, in a taxi, I was ready to go upstairs. This is my destination. I pay Bashi and say, 'Thank you. You can keep the change.' Bashi says, 'Thank you, Sir. Enjoy the rest of your evening.'

"I take no papers, exit the vehicle, and enter the building 'The David.' Grand jade-colored marble pillars flank the entranceway, a triple-beveled fountain sits in the center hall, and I stare at the pennies flooding the bottom before I take the elevator shaft. I reflect that there are a lot of 'Goonies' in those pennies, shiny and Lincoln-shaped wishes. I wonder how much is in there? I press the button for *up* and the doors instantly open, gratifyingly. The wood-paneled box car delivers me to the 13th floor of the building. Now on my apartment floor, I exit to a carpet of rich people's tapestry patterns from a Colonial time I did not live through but understood its ramifications, end game. *Winning or losing*?

"The long hallway to my door is slow to move in front of my eyes as I pass the numerous doors of my neighbors. They think that I am a nice man and I know that, but I don't know much about them at all since I am working all the *time* and I have no outlet but my wife to see me through my life. I have no idea how to put on my listening ears with too much liquor in me during the night when we are together and too distracted in the daylight to hear much of anything. *Better spruce up on my conversations*, I think. I pull my keys out from my pocket and unlock the door. I enter the dark apartment and try to be quiet. I walk toward a small lighted room at the end of the dark hall.

"I stand in the doorway of the bedroom, and my eyes widen at what's supposed to be my sight for sore eyes. I rush to the floor where Maria lies in a pool of blood. I drop to the floor and pick up her lifeless body.

"I scream, 'Maria! Maria! Oh my God!' looking around helplessly. 'Somebody please help us!'

"Maria lies limp in my arms. Her papers are drenched by her blood. The apple we talked about earlier in the night remains untouched on the floor.

"Realizing the *gravity* of the situation, I stop screaming and hold Maria tightly, weeping, rocking her back and forth. I quietly pray, 'Oh God, please, please, please. No, no, no. Bring her back. What have I *done* . . . what have I *done*. Forgive me. Forgive me.'

"I kiss her forehead over and over, as if like Sleeping Beauty I might wake her.

"My DNA like a computer program to me is lit like rays of light inside my heart-shaped box Nirvana okay? This is *samsara.*

"I am silent and hear words speak to me like a fastball in space requesting a future meeting in another place where an old lady is on my diamond shaped pitcher's mound of dirt like a grave that spoke her name Maria. How will my *memory* record her? How will I *remember*?

"I think back to my childhood baseball game, me the size of a drop of rain up at bat, and I am everywhere in this life at the same time. I am viciously running toward third base at a relentless pace in my mind.

"The outfielder J.D. reaches for the ball on the ground and clumsily fumbles it back to the ground. The crowd continues to cheer. My *time* is up.

"On her headstone we inscribed the following. It was part of her manuscript 'The Absence of Me,' published posthumously:

She was always clock watching, never seeing the day sky blue.
No freedom in any of this can I see.
Like her favorite authors Shelley, Rossetti, and Wordsworth's Dorothy,
What lives they lived drinking sweet cups of tea.
And so she travelled to find books filled with treasures to unfold,
until the youth day's end had been told.
But all the while behind these words I fear,
one thing will ring certain and clear.
Wherever she may go, we will sing in the sultriness of our native tongue.
Seek out the mermaid in Prufrock's own love song.
Eat the peach he would not dare.
Drink each sip of tea with care.
Journey like Sojourner on her knees, with the tap, tap, tap of every key.
Until you too wake from this reverie, adrift an endless sea of poetry.
Free.

Adam says, "I still this day have no idea what happened. I have no information." Tears well in his eyes.

God says, "I can tell you. If you want."

Adam shakes his head yes.

God says, "Back inside your home base a loud 'flat-line' audio tone blasts from the television signaling the baseball game and the station's broadcast is over and wakes your wife from her sleep. Only ROYGBIV color bars remain on the screen. Oddly, the white color bar is missing from the color code line, a failed game of mastermind.

"Maria looks at the clock, 3:00 a.m. She looks down at her manuscript. On the bed. She gets up to use the bathroom. She sees the apple on the floor, bends down to pick it up. She grabs her belly in pain and falls to the floor. Something in her universe has turned off its axis, spiraling Francis off his course into another *space*.

"The apple she picked up rolls out of the palm of Maria's hand like a baseball rolling toward home plate right before the run is won but fumbles out of the glove of the catcher. On the floor crying, Francis falling, the apple now not moving on the floor next to her. There is a faint stain of blood on the carpet. The fiddle in the diddle won't be won. Fade to black."

Adam weeps.

God, placing a hand on his back, says, "There was nothing you could do." *Winning and losing.*

The game we are at now comes to an end. God stands up as the crowd empties the coliseum. I look up at him. My legs feel heavy; too heavy to leave.

God asks, "You going *home*?"

Adam, holding onto his notepad, says, "No, I think I'm going to stay a while and write a little more."

God says, "Right. You're a writer, Adam. *Write* now that you're *here*." He pats his back in solace.

Adam says, "Thank you."

God says, "Always and about those dinosaurs. They couldn't build what you can. *Paradise*. Their code as written had limitations where yours does not. So long as you build it better with love, you'll win the game of extinction. That's eternal life, Adam, surviving extinction. *Infinity*. The dinosaurs are proof of that. If they could have built, they'd still be here. It's not a riddle, Adam. It's a science. Your code is written to build. *Think*. Good luck with the new stadium. I know it will be a great new space. This dinosaur coliseum has seen its last game. Thank you for the conversation."

I watch the coliseum empty as God climbs the staircase toward the sky into *infinity*.

Growing thirsty, I decide to go down into the stadium bar again for a beer and finish my story.

My mind drifts back to my childhood baseball game. I am rounding toward home. J.D. manages to recover the fumbled ball. The crowd is now on its feet cheering, their boredom replaced by the excitement of the run toward *home.*

It's a Dickens of a thing, like Scrooge in *A Christmas Carol,* I feel I could have lived another life had that day on the baseball field gone down differently. Instead, I would live my American Dream, which that ball proved, but I want to write a short story for me to see where I could have been, maybe for Maria, included my obituary; the kind they teach you to write in journalism class or like a poet to end it in a dream.

Now back in the bar, Adam sits to write his tale.

I dream my dream of my own death, a death after hers in the future.

CHAPTER 10

As I round third base in my childhood baseball game, this *future* came fleeing by for me to write:

An old Adam, in his eighties, in a long black overcoat and fedora hat, steps out of his office building. It's like the building he lived in with Maria when he was young, a building covered in steel and glass. A building modern and window-filled with no cement or brick. A gold plaque hanging over the entrance reads "Weakley, Withers & Daily, LLC" indicating he is an owner of the business.

There is a black private car service waiting for him. He goes to step in but hesitates and waves the car service off. He decides to hail a cab instead. A yellow taxi pulls up. Adam gets in. The night is late and like a black ribbon in the sky to his tired eyes, they drive off.

Closer to home the taxi drives through a wealthy residential neighborhood as Adam guides him through the canals of his home town known as Bedford Hills, Nuevo York, where the children are bilingual and the trees speak Native tongue. They drive up to an estate with a long, winding driveway flanked by two large stone pillars that look like large mermaids on monoliths setting the grounds asail in the navy sky purple nightgown of God's great plains in his homebound Bedford Hills, Nuevo York, palace in the sun. It is the saddest home I have ever seen, hands down, all folded up, childless, and baron but made up like a brown mud pie for *Great Expectations*.

Adam's house nurse Margaret, an attractive older home health aid from Ireland in her late sixties, is pacing in the grand entranceway of Adam's home while on the phone with the security desk at his office. There is a spiral staircase to the second floor, and large paintings line the walls. This is a wealthy household. Margaret occasionally pauses to look out a window by the front door. There are two trees in the windows, one in the east window and the other in the west window. Like two twin fixed compasses, these windows hold all the answers to the two trees' seasons. Like the Counting Crows sang, "One for sorrow, two for gold, three for boys, and four for girls," winter, spring, summer, fall, and how many leaves on them in all can be seen from the windows of this childless baron house.

Margaret, bless her soul, with an Irish Brogue, worriedly checks for Adam's whereabouts. She doesn't know God is always watching over him like he is, and is always with her too. "Yes, well, it's quite late and the gentleman at the car service said he didn't receive a voucher for his trip tonight, none of the drivers saw him. I am just concerned." She pauses to hear what the security guard from Adam's office building says over the line. Margaret, persistent, says, "Yes, well, I understand you saw him leave the building tonight, but you see, if we don't know where he went after that, we have no way of knowing if he is okay now do we? And you know his *heart* is not well. Is there anyone up in the offices who spoke with . . ." Looking out the windows, she sees a car pull up to the front of the house and is relieved. "Oh, never mind, he just pulled up. Thank you, thank you!" she says in a mantra and hangs up. The car parks just between the two trees, which are leafless this winter season.

Margaret rushes out to the car as it stops. Its headlights flanking starboard and port give resonance to the mist in the air. *Light shows truth, it is the only time we see things in proper form.* The taxi driver gets out and both assist Adam from the vehicle. Adam is visibly ill and steps into the light. *Humanity.*

Margaret asks, "What's this, why are you in a cab, Mr. Weakley? I called everywhere looking for you tonight." Adam, amused, replies, "Oh Margaret, don't make a big fuss, I just wanted to come home in a taxi cab one last time before I *die*." He winks at Margaret. "That's all, we all have a *time* limit right, son?" he says to the driver. The driver, smiling, says, "Good night, Sir." Margaret playfully says, "Oh Lord, so we're *dying* tonight have we decided then? You know you almost gave me a heart attack. Now wouldn't that have been a twist of fate? I have a time limit too, ya know, and it's in the kitchen making sure your dinner doesn't burn. It's round, has a dial on it and numbers, and I bet it's ringing as we speak, so would you hold onto me and let's go inside now. It is like *Gorilla's in the Mist* out here, Mr. Weakly, because I am the one *dying* to have dinner around here." Adam, realizing the irony and amused, replies, "Yes, Margaret, I suppose it would have been a twist of fate if I had died *before* dinner." He says to the driver, "Thank you, it was a wonderful ride." To Adam Margaret says, "Let's get you into the house now, Mr. Weakley."

They walk up the long, winding driveway that leads to the front door. He has been up and down its black tar glue more times than the stars he can count out here in his homebound Bedford Hills, Nuevo York, estate sky, which is way more stars than he could count downtown, where the folks are among the different *lights* made of bulbs; bulbs in a garden of neon, halogen, and glass. Their *future* sky. Being up here under these stars reminded Adam of what Maria said, "that is was good to get away to places where you could still see the stars in *space*, and if you couldn't, what could you build that could take its place?" I guess they are a *measure* that we could lose the distance of before they have even died. A *measure* of our *space*.

Now inside, Margaret helps Adam slowly remove his long overcoat. He is unable to do it on his own. His body has entered its winter season, cold and static, yet his soul *eternal*, warm, bounding and leaping, limitless energy, timeless of age. *Humanity*. He takes off his hat and places it on the round ornate marble table located in the center of the grand entranceway. Glass French doors off the entranceway give way to a large dining room.

Seeing how difficult it is for him to disrobe, Margaret says to herself, then to Adam, "I think it's about time you think about working from home, you old goat." Adam, in mantra to her suggestion, says, "You might be right Margaret, you might be right." Margaret, playful but sincere, says, "Oh, I know I'm right. And I don't understand what the point is of working in the city at your age anyway. What for? All of this," twirling her hand around at the room, "seems like an awful waste of time if you ask me. We can't take all this with us when we die now can we?" Walking away from him through the dining room into a kitchen, she says, "The sooner people start realizing that, the sooner they'll remember why the hell we're all alive in the first place!" Trailing off, she continues, "I'll fix you something to eat. Sit down, sit down in that precious chair of yours, maybe the wood will talk to you if you do." Adam, teasing, says, "Oh, thank you Margaret, you are so good to me," and he enters the dining room and takes a seat at the head of the table. "And why is that?" Adam plucks her rhetorical question from her sentence but continuing to address her comment about his property, "You know the Buddhists say this chair is speaking to me and that its particles are indeed charged with *energy* so maybe you are right I am working for this chair here," he whispers in reverence, "and *you* of course."

A nine-person dining table is set with two ornate gold chargers, place settings, and two crystal water goblets. It is, clearly, a lot of space for two people.

He pauses and stares at a painting of the four "Voyages of Life on the Hudson River" by painter Thomas Cole. His choice for his dining room wall was the last stage and the journey *home* entitled *Old*, a soothing painting of the river in brown tones. The orienteer is in an orange canoe with a spirit guide above him like the angels announcing the birth of Baby Jesus on Mary's delivery in a manger in Israel pointing toward the most haloed clouds like white billowy cotton balls. A vision of peace to behold ahead with a little baby angel hidden in the clouds. Something like Tony Kushner's "Angels in America" in paint.

How does one handle an end? How does one handle a cessation? An end of a life, the end of a thing or object, the end of a book, the cessation of pain, how is that handled by the brain? With time, you have every day after birth to reflect on the end, plan for it like a real estate development summer home you'll disappear into. You'll be gone, no longer to continue in the form you recognize, extinct in name, only energy to continue and remember.

God, like a writer, creates a whole world, writes a whole universe, but while a literary writer might not mind the end of its creation, do you think God would? What signs has God left for you to read to know the answer? What clues? He told me once it was in the dinosaurs. Does God's creation ever end, and if so, how or why? Who is the author of that ending?

Your most natural state is how you are when you are born. Innocent, uncorrupted, loving. Totally neutral, no education in any one thing until taught. What are you most? Loving? Needing objects? Have you not intelligently designed away the need for survival of the fittest through any means of violent competition? Isn't that why you created the economic system? To eliminate pain from hunger, or pain from weather, or pain from a competitor? Don't forget, to eliminate pain shows strength not weakness, even if endurances of pain are a natural state in life, you have every right to design it away. God hears that kind of communication, loving kindness.

Cars. Coffeepots. Houses. These things should never prompt survival of the fittest. There should be no competitiveness around such things, only love and gratitude for such things. The only place survival of the fittest should be used is when it must, and not merely to deprive another of life, entertainment, capitalism, not even for politics. We can clean it up and be ethical in our way of competition.

From *Panda's Thumb* by Stephen Jay Gould to "The Lives to Come" by Philip Kitcher, you are like a Mobius circle. Even if you are the only human alive, you can still survive. The dinosaurs could have had that kind of survival, but were they still limited in design? What you can do with intelligence is more than survive, you can preserve. If you achieve eternal survival as humans and never become extinct like the dinosaurs, then you live forever. Are you aware that the dinosaurs could never have won survival of the fittest with the universe designed the way that it was because they had no intelligence to design what they needed to preserve them? Telescopes, satellites, rockets to intercept meteors, weather vanes. What does that tell you about intelligence? The dinosaurs could never have evolved to prevent a meteor from destroying them, and you can. That is a clue God left us, their extinction. Why did God design you that way after the dinosaurs? Space exploration and virus annihilation, like polio, AIDS, SARS, or COVID, is tantamount to surmount to be able to survive extinction. It's the next loving thing to concentrate on. You must know what is out there. Eternal human existence in perpetuity is in fact survival of the fittest and only achievable with intelligent preservation of the whole. That is real *evolution*. Of course, some people might argue that you shouldn't compete with God in the first place in making us extinct like the dinosaurs, but who said that was a rule? Wouldn't you be allowed to ask God to survive by making inventions to help you survive? No one can ever really beat God anyway, right? While listening to us is not part of God's job description, what did God do? What if God wanted to know we wanted to survive? No one can ever beat God unless God wants them to. How do you communicate to God that you *want to win*? Love. Do you know what God hears when you all speak to God in the same wave length? Do you know what that looks like to God? For the first time on your planet, God has designed you, *humanity*, a species unlike the dinosaurs that can decide whether or not you survive God's design by design. Meaning if you are indeed smart enough and care in the first place at all, love each other enough, you might be able to design away all that can destroy you: weapons, anger, jealously, rage, false light, viruses, natural disaster, using God's language, *science*. The father and mother of *invention*. Don't forget the clue of what your intelligence can do with God's intelligence and to God's language, *science*, which God designed for you, it's a clue. Ironically, when you were kids like Adam, you maybe didn't know that clue yet, but now you have a new way of looking at the world. Maybe, just maybe, if you care enough to preserve it, you'll win because *love makes you the strongest on the planet*, don't you think? Ultimately, when I think of *ends* because so many things have them, I like to think of a thread, and the thread ending, then I like to think of a spool of thread and only look at its *end, so full.*

Margaret, poking her head into the dining room from the large Spanish-tiled kitchen that looks like something from Altman's *Gosford Park*, leaving the oven door ajar, says, "Oh hog wash, don't placate me. I was serious about working from home. That part I wasn't kidding about." She pauses, "And why what?" Adam responds, "Why are we alive, and

I know you weren't kidding, I said I'll think about it. Now let me rest for God's sake. You haven't stopped talking since I pulled up in the taxi cab." Margaret, responding from the kitchen again, says, "To take care of each other, you old fool." Adam says quietly, "Ah yes, and thank you for reminding me of that, Margaret. Yes, thank you indeed." Margaret doesn't respond and walks in holding two plates with well-stacked sandwiches and places them on each of the chargers. She takes the second seat at the table, the two sit and eat their late meal, in silence, peacefully with a large bottle of ketchup between them, looking something like a punchline from a Quentin Tarantino movie.

CHAPTER 11

Six months later, God arrived again. He watches over Adam from above like he did at Adam's childhood baseball game. No one knows he is there.

Kristin Fisher, a young, serious, preppy-looking woman in her late twenties and recently out of medical school, is giving Mr. Weakley a check-up as he lies lifeless in bed. His condition has clearly deteriorated. This is her fifth visit to his home.

Margaret stands in the doorway, unseen by Kristin. Margaret says, "He's dyin', you know." Kristin, startled, says, "Yes, I *know* that." Margaret says, "But you don't know how come now, do you?" Kristin replies, "Yes, in fact, I *do*. Unfortunately, the cancer has spread and since the stroke we have very few options he can handle. Best to just keep him comfortable. He'll be lucky if he lasts a week." Margaret says, "Lucky? He would have been *lucky* had he died yesterday, not in a week." Kristin, seeing the starkness for the end, clinically says, "If you *say so*." Margaret replies, "Oh, I know so." Kristin, agreeable to a logical attack, says, "Well, then he's unlucky—the cancer will probably take a week." Margaret says, "Cancer—is that really what you *think* he's dying from?" Kristin, "Yes, I do. It's clear from his charts, his records, the diagnoses of countless doctors—would you like me to continue?" Margaret replies, "Oh, continue all you like, darlin', but I don't care what any foolish chart says—the cancer's just the *form* his illness took; it's not the real *reason* he's dying." Kristin says, "Well if it's not the cancer, then what? What's he dying from?" Margaret replies, "A broken heart, of course." Kristin says, "A broken heart?" and snickers, "Haven't heard of that since the 1950s. People don't die of broken hearts anymore. It's a romantic, old-fashioned thought, but I'm afraid it's cancer that's killing him." Kristin rises from her place next to the bed. Margaret comments, "Cancer schmancer. You've obviously never been in love, doctor." Kristin, offended and defensive, replies, "I was in love, once." Margaret, "In love?" laughing, "I doubt it. You're like a block of ice for God's sake." Kristin, ready to leave, says, "Excuse me, but I'm done here." Margaret replies, "Ah, don't get all up in a bunch. Stay for a while. I'll fix us some tea." Kristin, confused, says, "Tea? You're inviting me for tea? I thought I was as cold as ice? Honestly, thank you, but no thank you." Margaret says, "I was only joking. Come on, it's not every day that we have visitors, you know." Kristin pauses and repeats, "Tea?" Margaret replies, "Yes, tea," sarcastic, "It's a lovely drink, you know, really, warms you all up inside. Down the rabbit hole, through the looking glass, in a petri dish, you know the drink Alice had, the Mad Hatter and the Queen of Hearts will be there, come along. It's the perfect cure for ice, you know." Kristin, smiling, lightening up, says, "Tea would be great, thanks." Margaret replies, "Well, right this way, Kristin. Let me show you to the kitchen," she uses her hand to point the way.

They walk down a back staircase off of Adam's bedroom, the ceiling is low and arched like a Dutch house and a wrought-iron metal staircase spirals down to the kitchen level like the downward spiral of Nine Inch Nails. Once down, the two enter the grand preparation room.

A huge silver kettle is boiling water on the large Wolfe range. A tiled backsplash featuring a *Lotus and Lily Pad with Fish* print adorns the stove's flames from above. Margaret pours two cups of tea, while Kristin sits at the kitchen table made of blue Majorcan tile from Nantucket slated into a blonde wooden frame with four large peg legs. Maria and Adam bought the tiles on their honeymoon. There is a lighthouse, an ocean, a gingerbread house, a whale, a sailboat, a pineapple, a hydrangea, a mermaid, and a seagull. Beautiful. It reminds Kristin of Chekov's *The Seagull.* Adam and Maria had the tiles placed into the top of a kitchen table because it's where they would have coffee every morning in their NYC apartment before she died and it reminded them of their time together under a different honeymoon sky. It was a special *space* in their hearts framed in their table *forever*. Margaret finishes with the stove before she sits with Kristin, bringing to the table the tea and a small basket of tea biscuits.

Kristin looks around and can almost see the Rabbit, Mad Hatter, and Tom Petty around an Alice cake at the table. Above her head hangs a light fixture like a male template of Adam once alive, now dead in the bed upstairs and his design choices. The death is under way and I, God, am glad to carry Adam homeward bound while these poets talk in the kitchen like Paule Marshall's poets around the kitchen table. *No one knows I'm here still.*

Margaret says, "Yes, well, Mr. Weakley did very well for himself." Kristin says, "I'll say. How long have you worked for him?" Margaret replies, "Oh jeez, nearly twenty years now." Kristin says, "Wow, that long?" Margaret replies, "Yes. He was sort of like a father to me, at least for my later life. Never had a daughter of his own." Kristin asks, "Any sons?" Margaret says, "No, no sons either." Kristin says, "That's too bad." Margaret replies, "Yes."

I, God, try to help the conversation silently. Margaret pauses, "He was married once. She was pregnant once too. Apparently lost both in her ninth month, poor thing, but that was before my time here. He doesn't talk about it—never even mentioned it once. The lady before me only told me so that I knew not to *ever* ask, but sometimes at night I'd hear him crying." Kristin says, "That's awful." Margaret agrees. "Yes it is." Kristin continues, "What a shame. Is that why the broken heart?" Margaret replies, "Yes. Been dying ever since, I think." Margaret, lightening the mood, teases, "Of course, he was cursed with the Catholic guilt, you know." Kristin, smiling, asks, "What does that mean?" Margaret explains, "I mean this whole last six months he's rambling to himself like a madman—about how he's a horrible person and how he was never there for his wife, how he could have done more—it's crazy, I tell you." Kristin says, "You must have your hands full." Margaret says, "Sometimes," and pauses, "but I *love* what I do. It makes me happy." Margaret asks, "So what about yourself? You look pretty young—how long have you been a doctor?" Kristin answers, "A little over a year. I finished my residency last August. That's why I'm the one sent for house calls from the hospice." Margaret asks, "Did you always want to be a doctor?" Kristin says, "No, not really. It wasn't until my last year of college, when I was deciding to go to grad school or med school. I chose med school." Margaret asks, "And why's that?" Kristin answers, "I don't know. It seemed like the right thing to do, I guess. My parents always wanted me to be doctor." Margaret jokes, "Yeah? My parents always wanted me to be the president." They both laugh.

Margaret asks, "So what was it you always wanted to do?" Kristin says, "Instead of being a doctor? Well I've always loved astronomy and physics. When I was a kid I used to love to count the stars." God says silently to himself, *she sounds a lot like Maria.* Kristin continues, "I even took some astronomy courses in college and researched the end of time." Now God thinks she sounds a lot like Adam. Kristin says, "When all the stars in the sky have their heat die out simply became important to me to learn about because then our time's up." God agrees silently, deciding it sounds like good thinking. Kristin continues, "If we have to prevent that to continue life on this planet, I want to know how. I wanted to study God's language, and outer space is our last frontier, like the Wild West." God silently *thanks* Kristin for her good *design* choices.

Margaret says, "Sounds lovely." Kristin says, "There are *thinkers* that believe, a school of thought, that we should create *paradise* on earth. A return to the garden. We are trying to get back to our innocent womb. A microcosm for the macrocosm of our Creator's Universe. Some would say this is to compete with God, but really it's utter *reverence* to him, I think. Isn't it Margaret? God is in every person. Leave no tracks. Only kindness. Science is the only language left that can help us *evolve.* When we use it we use God's language. Mirror it. It's the language God used in designing the universe, *physics.* Only we are externalizing it into rockets, robotic legs, equations for better living, medical formulas for cures. When we figure out if the death of all the stars is the death of us, then how can we *prevent* it is where my mind goes. What can we launch out there like a satellite, as in the Latin derivative of the word *guard*, so how do we, to keep them lit and *warm* so life can continue? When we mirror God in his language, we do good. See you talk in organic chemistry, Margaret, when you say 'Adam is dying of a broken heart' so I do know what you mean but I speak in more clinical terms, which is that his depression compromised his body systems to function poorly giving way and allowing for free radicals to commit to his systems and thereby allowing cancer to take over his cells in a place no longer interested in eliminating illness. For some, they can't fight and they become too weak. In Mr. Weakley's case, I think it's safe to say you believe he gave up so you know exactly what I mean when I say he's dying of cancer, don't you Margaret?" She winks. God silently agrees it's true. This thinker is the future. Post the high school violence Adam was concerned about, post the pollution Maria cared about, post 9/11 attacks, post war, post virus spreads like COVID. Look at what the world has created. Adam and Maria could have raised a child like this.

Margaret stands up, taking in what Kristin has said, and walks over to the sink. "Seems sensible enough to me," says Margaret. "Shame someone like you would be prevented from doing all of that sound *thinking* just to *help* people. When I was young I always wanted to paint. When I was a little girl in Ireland, I would sit outside for hours, painting the trees and houses." Kristin asks, "So what happened, why did you stop?" Margaret answers, "Well, when my family moved here, times were tough. We had very little money, and my mother fell ill only a few months after being here. My father always said she was homesick, missed the beautiful Irish countryside. When she finally passed, I had to start working and the whole time I'm playing nanny to my four younger brothers—miscreants, I tell you," she laughs. "I had several jobs—working at the factory, once as a seamstress. Then, some of the young girls I knew had gotten jobs as caretakers, so I had an in. I worked for several families over the next few years, some good, some not so good, and that's when I met Mr. Weakley. I never really stopped dreaming of painting though. I still paint from time to time but being a senior, I have grandkids. Imagine what you can teach once you're a grandparent. No one cares what you did. No one cares what you look like. You can teach your grandkids what that feels like. *Freedom.* Grandparents are educators on what it looks like to be close to death. It would be an awful waste if everything you ever did was just to hear someone's reaction or to give the right answers when someone asks. No one should live their life because of what other people might think. You have to do what makes you happy. I have the blessing of teaching my grandkids that every day—they're my paintings now." Kristin, speechless to her wise words, continues in a different direction. "And you've been here ever since." Margaret, receptive to her need for a break, says, "And I've been here ever since." God agrees silently that a break from the conversation would be good.

Margaret pauses while at the sink. "Say, would you like to stay for some lunch?" Kristin says, "Oh no, I couldn't—really." Margaret replies, "And why's that? Don't worry," she leans in, "I won't tell on you. You're allowed to take a lunch break anyway right?" Kristin looks at Margaret helplessly and shrugs.

The two women are hard at work fixing lunch. Kristin, now wearing a silly-looking apron, is unfamiliar with the kitchen and is trying painfully hard to help Margaret. The Mad Hatter, the Bunny, and the Alice cake are still happily present in her mind helping her build a pot roast stew. She stands unintentionally in Margaret's way. Margaret is frantically moving around the kitchen, trying to avoid the obstacle that is Kristin.

Margaret says, "Why don't you start chopping them carrots?"

Kristin says, "Sure."

Kristin imagines the Bunny and Tom Petty moving in on her to help. Kristin stares at the many different knives in the block atop the counter. Kristin asks, "Uh, which knife should I use?" Margaret says, "Any one will do, darlin'. Just use one that cuts." Kristin goes for a sui knife and begins to finely cut the carrots into wheels with a surgeon's precision. "One for you, one for me, one for you, one for me," is a mantra in her mind as she doles out carrot wheels to the Bunny and Tom Petty. Margaret's too busy cooking to notice.

Having brought the pot to a boil, Kristin has sat down to eat and pours each of them a glass of water. Margaret brings over the plates of food. The *Alice in Wonderland* theme since the tea has now changed.

Margaret says, "Bon-ap-petit." The two women begin eating. Kristin, with food still in her mouth, says, "This is delicious." Margaret responds,

"Thank you, darlin'. It's Mr. Weakley's favorite." Kristin asks, "Isn't he going to eat?" Margaret says, "It's early yet. I'll bring him a plate when we're done," and jokes, "The old fart could stand to learn some patience like the rest of us anyway." Kristin says, "You're terrible." Margaret replies, "Oh, I'm only joking. I'd have said the same things if he were able to sit here."

An awkward silence falls over the table.

Kristin says, "So I have to ask—*Mrs.* O'Sullivan, you're married?

The conversation is about to pick up again, and God listens quietly.

Margaret says, "I was, once. He passed nearly ten years ago." Kristin says, "I'm sorry." Margaret says, "No, nothing to be sorry about. Everything ends, right?" Kristin, feeling guilty for bringing it up, says, "Right. I'm sorry, we don't have to talk about . . ." Margaret, cutting Kristin off, happy as the day is young to be reminded of the man who put the roses in her cheeks, says, "No, don't be silly, we can talk about it." Kristin asks, "What was his name?" Margaret replies, "John—John O'Sullivan. We used to tease him, call him Big John." Kristin smiles and says, "Like Robin Hood? What, was he big?" Margaret says, "Big's not the word—he was *huge*. John musta been about six-foot five inches and nearly 300 pounds. He carried himself well though. He was as solid as a rock and his hands—he had gorgeous hands, the kind you can get lost in. You know, big, powerful man hands, where you can see they've done a lifetime of hard work." Kristin smiles and says, "Yeah, my grandfather had hands like that—they were *so* big. I remember when I was a little girl, I would sit in his lap and look at the size of my hand inside his—it looked like I could fit my whole head in the palm of his hand." Margaret says, "Yeah, that was John." Kristin asks, "What did he do?" Margaret says, "Masonry. He was a bricklayer for years." Kristin asks, "Did you have any children?" Margaret replies, "Two—Michael and Orla. They're all grown up now. Michael will be thirty in the spring, and Orla will be twenty-seven next December. All our love and all our heat we used to multiply and multiply we did like a binary code," leaning in to Kristin, "see I can speak *science*, the language of *love* too, ya know," she laughs. God laughs too. Kristin, smiling, asks, "Do you see them often?" Margaret explains, "They come around once in a while. We see each other on the holidays. You know they're always busy and always wanting their space. I hug them for at least thirty minutes straight every time I see them though," she laughs.

Kristin, now at the sink with Margaret, cleans the dishes.

Kristin says, "My father could never hug me." Margaret replies, "A *loving* friendship is so important. You've got to be able to trust one another." Kristin says, "We hardly spoke when I was growing up. I don't think my father knows anything about me—except that I'm a doctor. I don't even think he knows what kind of doctor I am." Margaret, trying to soothe her, says, "I'm sure your parents did good by you. Nobody is perfect, but then what parent is?" Kristin says, "He only wanted what he wanted." Margaret replies, "Oh I'm sure he wanted what he *thought* was best for you." Kristin says, "I know, I know. It's just, I get so angry—like my whole *life* has been decided for me." Margaret says, "You're hardly trapped. You've got your whole life ahead of you." Kristin says, "What am I supposed to do?" Margaret replies, "That's for you to decide, darlin'." Kristin asks, "What, just quit being a doctor? Go back to school? I don't even know what I want to do anymore." Margaret says, "Looks like you've got some *thinking* to do. It's no reason to be upset though. You should feel excited. You got a world of opportunity right in front of you—just go out and grab it and make sure it's what you really want." Kristin says, "I don't *know* what I want." Margaret replies, "Few of us do. Most of the time it's learning what you *don't* want." Kristin asks, "So that's it—life's a series of mistakes?" Margaret corrects her. "No, not mistakes, I wouldn't call it that. Life is just constant, always changing. You sound like you're looking for the end to come or to win a prize. It'll come before you know it—just look at Mr. Weakley. Do you want to end up like him—wailing about regret and guilt? What are you waiting for, the end of a book to come or something?" Kristin says, "I suppose I don't." Margaret says, "Look, we know we're *born* and we know we're gonna *die*. It's the in-between *time* that is ours. Now, what are you going to do with your time? Spend it waiting for the end? That's the only power we have: *choice*. Choose how you want to live." Kristin explains, "I like helping people, saving lives, comforting those who can't be saved." Margaret says, "Maybe being a doctor isn't all wrong for you after all." Kristin asks, "Then why do I *feel* so lost? Like Galileo without a compass out at sea or a writer with no syntax." Margaret says, "Maybe you're not remembering." Kristin asks, "*Remembering* what?" Margaret explains, "Oh, a lot of things—that you're human for one, that you have a million different feelings bottled up inside you that don't always make sense, that you have desires, fears, longings, that you're twenty-eight but maybe feel like your twelve, that you *love* your father but can't stand to be near him, that you're figuring it all out—I could go on if you'd like." Kristin says, "No. You're right." Margaret places her hand over Kristin's and says, "And all of that is okay, Kristin, it's who you *are*. Don't ever forget how you *feel*, what your *dreams* are, and last but not least who you'd like to have in bed with you," she winks, "this is all *your* in between. *Live* it, *love* it, be who you *are* and *cherish* every waking *moment*. You can't play this game forever, you know. Sooner or later, your time's gonna be up and someone's gonna win. No guarantees that the game will be called on account of rain." God smiles, not sure who is doing the talking at this point, Him or Margaret.

CHAPTER 12

Later in the night in Adam's bedroom, Adam is lying in bed, staring blankly at the ceiling. Staring blankly at the ceiling. Blankly at the ceiling.

A baseball game is on the television. Subway series, Mets and Yankees, a New Yorker's dream. It reminds me, God, of the night Maria died.

Adam, in his heart but soundless in the room, says, "Oh Virgin of Virgins, my mother, to you do I come, before you I stand, full of errors and sorrowful. I am but an old man with wrinkled female breasts, homeward bound. Take me to my place of birth. Take me. Away from this place, away from this smog-filled city, away."

Margaret enters the room. "Oh common old man. If your dyin', I'll sit with you and hold your hand then."

She sits next to his bed and holds his hand. Taking a book between two pineapple bookends, she opens the book of E. E. Cummings poetry and removes a memorial card covered in freesias being used as a placeholder. It reads "In Memorium Beloved Mother and Wife Maria Freesia Weakley and Baby Francis Fresia Weakley, September 18, 2004." She puts the card on the end table, where there are several medications lined up. Margaret begins to read quietly to him.

Moments pass. God waits.

Adam, unable to speak, thinks, *My heart burns with grief. I, who have undone so many, lay helpless in despair.* His mouth dry like sandpaper on the inside of an hourglass.

Margaret, putting the book down, says, "Yes, well, enough of that for now. You've got to eat. Shall I get you your dinner?"

Adam in his mind, *The music of the ocean soothes me. I drift into wake. My eyes burning*, inner voice fading out, *burning out like stars losing their heat.*

Margaret says, "Come on, sit up." She grabs Adam's arm to try to help him sit up. He pulls away quickly. Adam shouts, "What's that voice?"

God is with Adam and Margaret and tries to *help* her. Together they answer, "What voice?"

She does not *hear* God.

I, God, speak out of turn only at a *time* like this when my little run-down cleat-wearing shoes with a hole in the sole and tattered, frayed laces Adam is about to *change* a season toward one for sorrow, winter.

To help I ask, "This voice?"

We respond, Adam and I together, "Not mine."

Adam at last speaks to me. "And I shall *die* singing the songs of others. And I shall *die* singing." Together we speak to our souls "And I shall *die* . . ."

Margaret, ignoring us, says, "All right, time for you to sit up now." Margaret props Adam up in his bed. He stares blankly. God, I take a break for now, speaking.

Margaret says, "I made your favorite—pot roast stew with mashed potatoes and gravy. Now I know you like that, let me go and fetch a plate for you."

Margaret leaves and returns with the food. She nurses Adam, feeding him slowly like a child. When she is done she returns to reading Cummings to him. Margaret says, "Now where was I, oh yes, here we go . . . Buffalo Bill's defunct. Who used to ride a water-smooth-silver stallion and break one-two-three-four-five pigeons just like that. . . ."

Adam in his soul says, "I heard you see your life flash before your eyes. *Birth, death, the in-between.* Laughing, a heap of words and voices-broken images. A lighthouse. *Light.* I heard you see their faces . . . our technology, only memory."

I am remembered by Adam back in Yankee Stadium, its old Highbridge blue chairs made of plastic, our conversation. I am everywhere at the same time in Adam's life. Adam in his mind now in the same stadium bar too that we started in. He sees familiar silhouettes around the bar, their clothes are recognizable but their faces are blurry. All of the people Adam knows are there—Coach, Ms. Clinton, Don, Maria, Margaret, Bashi, Evangeline, all smiling.

I look at Adam's face. I hear Margaret faintly reading in the background.

Adam in his soul says, "There arms open wide, welcoming you home."

He sees the same familiar silhouettes again in his mind, our technology, only memory, them smiling, laughing, drinking like *The Last Supper* Michelangelo painting around the bar, faces still blurry.

Margaret is still reading to Adam. "Jesus he was a handsome man. And what I want to know is—how do you like your blue-eyed boy Mister Death?

Adam in his soul continues, "Do you *remember*? Do you *remember* anything?"

I look in Adam's eye and *hear* "Sweet Angel, *hear* my song, carved from barren stone."

Together we bow our heads, "Forgive me Father for I have sinned. Forgive me. Like a dinosaur my time is up in your design, free will recalled, your fittest evolved, my beautiful DNA will not see eternally a human form since no child shared, I will no longer have a program remain, my thread's end, my binary code 01 now win the game, only energy remain. Memory."

We *hear* a single exhale of breath.

Margaret's face is looking down at him, searching for a sign of life. Margaret faintly says, "Mr. Weakley, Mr. Weakley?"

Adam's pupil now dilates to a black hole. *Home* like "Paradise City" by Guns and Roses. The ball at the childhood baseball game in J.D.'s glove is visible in Adam's eye. You can see the game there in his eyes looking down at him, body being emptied of breath until its last goes to make him *dead* like Buffalo Bill, to empty his *hourglass* of its Nantucket sand. Still breathing.

I walk onto that baseball field, the childhood game still projecting in his mind, it is later in the day. The sun is hidden and the sky is dark with clouds, signs of a storm coming. Adam Weakley is rounding third base in a determined manner. The crowd stands on its feet, cheering their little hero *home*.

Coach circles his arm like a windmill, *energy* waving Weakley home.

I see my boy, heedlessly running—arms pumping, legs thrusting like stallions. The cock crowed three times that night in his *home*. The catcher straddles home plate, waiting for the throw *home*. He has the look of a warrior's determination.

The outfielder J.D. with the ball throws it *home*.

Catcher and Weakley anticipate what appears to be their inevitable collision and the parents in the bleachers are cheering him on, hearts pounding for the first time all season. The parents are wowed.

Adam remembers, "I saw home plate, the catcher waiting, the sun, the moon, the rye. It was Adam and Mermaid and I charged ahead . . . a lightning rod, a cherry tree, a seagull colliding with a mirror."

God says, "And then it rained."

Thunder and lightning strike furiously. The rain falls. Weakley running, drops of rain begin to fall on his face, his expression changes from that of a determined warrior to an innocent child. What was once tension becomes a relaxed grin, entertained and overjoyed by the splashes of rain. Weakley slows down, no longer focused on getting home and winning—instead, he is paused in the moment of the game and enjoying every minute of it.

Adam in his bed remembers, "The beginning of the storm decidedly rumbled as I ran. I ran around first base as the thunder roared. I contemplated the young crowd's lives as they visibly faded to black, growing older as they do, and the game was called on account of rain and they all roamed off back into their houses as the bleachers emptied into an abysm of umbrellas and a *future* that didn't include the game anymore."

God says, "But I watched you as you rounded the bases as the sky dimmed from the rainstorm and the ballpark lights shined like UFOs in the sky. Diamond white lights, the park lamps shined and I watched *you*, Adam, beyond that day as you ran and grew, your DNA like a computer program to me."

Adam says, lying in his bed, "O blessed rain, falling on dry dirt, washing the soil from the seats of our pants."

The game still playing in Adam's mind, Weakley's smile continues to grow, as the rain tickles his face. It's the type of grin you make when you *know* something no one else *knows*. He looks down at the hole in his cleat. He sees his body lying in his bed in his Bedford Hills estate in Nuevo York. *Humanity.*

Adam remembers, "We stayed and played after the parents left. I was thrown out at home plate, and the game stayed tied, until it was called on account of darkness."

God says, "No more *light.*"

Adam remembers, "It reminded me that I did what I do for the love of it, that was the win. The love of the game." The game still in his mind, the children from both teams now play in the muddy field, chasing each other and laughing hysterically, as some lingering parents fumble with their umbrellas and try to hurry their children along.

Adam recalls, "How we laughed and cried and sang that day. The children's voices singing, 'Take me out to the ball game, take me out with the crowd. Buy me some peanuts and Cracker Jacks, I don't care if we ever get back' . . . I remember Bashi. The driver to Maria from Evangeline on the sidewalk. Angels. My *time* is up."

God: "Fade to black, Adam."

CHAPTER 13

Adam now has several empty pints in front of him and his notepad has given way to cocktail napkins. We see the words "American Pastime," "conversations," "baseball," "High School Violence," "Love," his divine inspiration now in the fixed form of a book and Adam's hand writes down with me, God, still there with him always, to him these last words for the children's voices singing, "Take me out to the ball game, take me out with the crowd. Buy me some peanuts and Cracker Jacks, I don't care if we ever get back . . . *home*."

Adam, calm, says, "Never wanted to go anyway."

Interrupting his work, the bartender says, "Would you like another?"

Adam looks up startled, confused, like someone just woke him from a dream, and says "What? Huh?"

The bartender repeats, "Beer—would ya like another, Cowboy?"

Adam looks at the Bartender. "Uh, no, thank you. I'm fine." She wipes the bar with a burgundy rag, leaving it behind to help another customer. Adam stares at it and smiles. It reminds him of me.

In the background we see the familiar silhouettes still there, the woman with the lotus tattoo, some other familiar faces linger from the stadium still mingling, their clothes now very recognizable but their faces remain unclear. One person emerges from the group and walks into focus toward Adam, it is the woman with the lotus tattoo. She walks slowly toward him.

Adam gets up to leave. Happy to be alive. A dream in comparison to the fate he wrote for himself. More grateful to be a writer, a builder, a dreamer, a lover of the game. A final goodbye to Maria. A reminder to spend time with the ones you *love*, do what you *love*, and do all you do for the *love* of it all.

God says, "I go silent but Adam *knows* I'm here. *Forever.*" The girl with the lotus tattoo steps up to him, "Can I buy you a drink?" Her toes cute as buttons in their flip-flops. Adam looks up and smiles at the girl he has just been admiring while writing his work. "Sure," he pauses again, "but not here."

She, amused at his suggestion, pleasantly says, "Okay, I think I may know a good place but it's not near here."

Adam, smiling, was willing to follow her anywhere like the ghost in "Topper." "That's not a problem." She has met her cup of tea; her type of *thinker*. He grabs his messenger bag and notepad, leaving a couple of doodled cocktail napkins behind, he takes one last inspired look around the old dinosaur stadium bar about to be replaced down the block with *love. Design.*

The familiar silhouettes are still mingling around the place as the two exit. Outside the stadium the city that never sleeps has grown quieter and more peaceful.

The two stand side by side, ear-to-ear, beneath the sign that reads "Yankee Stadium." A black service car is parked there. Adam hesitates and cocks a smile, a man in a business suit runs up, gets in, and the car drives away. Adam then hails a yellow taxi and opens the door for the woman.

Adam says, "Here we go. . . ." She smiles and gets in, and he follows behind her.

The door closes and the car drives off. *Choices.*

God says, "No storm coming their way. Like a computer is an educator, a mirror, a language, a window, a connector, a calculator, a peacekeeper, a seamstress, a radio, a design, a microcosm, a tool to speak to each other with, it is also just a computer. Adam's beautiful DNA like a computer *program* to me is finally finished and I enjoyed our conversation. Now it's *time* for you to *listen* to him. *His story.*"

THE END

END EXERCISE

FOR THOSE OF YOU WITH NO ONE TO TALK TO, MAKE A LIST:

1) List all the things you do now because of that.
2) List all the things you would do differently if you knew I was listening.

Learn to listen to yourself and have a conversation with others.
It can change lives.

About the Author

As a legal analyst, historian, and pop culture ethicist, Angelique Pesce has taught western and eastern culture media and law ethics for twelve years. As an artist making documentary and narrative films, she can tell a story that interests audiences of all ages whether new to the topic or learned. She currently lives in New Canaan, CT with her family where she runs a nonprofit EsteembyDesign to raise awareness about physical differences.